WERERAT

Jonathan P. Brazee

Wererat

Semper Fi Press

Copyright © 2012 Jonathan P. Brazee

ISBN-13: 978-0615817880 (Semper Fi Press)
ISBN-10: 0615817882
ASIN: B008IE9HG8

Printed in the United States of America

The scream erupted from deep inside of him despite his determined intentions, echoing within the Pit.

The pain receded slightly, allowing Rafe to open his eyes. His heart was pounding as he gulped in deep breaths. That air almost made him gag, though. He looked down at his naked, sweat-covered body, and to his shame, saw that he had fouled himself, sending shit to join the vomit on the rough stone floor, vomit he had previously spewed even before the pain had gotten too intense.

Mortified that he was being observed, he sat up and put his back against the wall, hands covering his crotch, waiting for the next attack. His body still ached, but that was peanuts compared to the agony of his body being torn apart as each wave washed over him.

He looked up the walls of the Pit to the grate-covered opening some 30 feet above him. Moonlight already lit the top couple of feet of one side of the round walls, but Rafe could not yet directly see the moon itself.

The next wave began to manifest itself, and a small cry escaped his lips. He didn't know how much longer he could take it. He fell over to the floor in the fetal position, arms clasped around his stomach. The pain started slowly, centered in his gut. For a moment, it began to recede, and Rafe looked up, daring to hope that it was over. But that was a feint. The full brunt of the piercing agony exploded in his gut, then took hold of his spine, wrenching it, tearing it apart. Rafe didn't even attempt to hold back. He let loose his despair, not caring who watched him, who heard him.

He wasn't even aware of when it began to ebb away again. He slowly began to be cognizant of his pulse, of his face against the rough stone floor, of the smells of vomit, shit, and rancid sweat. He turned his look upwards, and just at the lip of the opening, the edge of the moon could be seen. He looked at it dully, almost with resentment, where only a short time before, the moonrise had filled him with nervous excitement.

Jonathan P. Brazee

He didn't bother to move as he watched more and more of the moon edge into view. He had been somewhat embarrassed to be stripped and shoved into the pit by the others, to know they were observing him. But now, none of that mattered. He only watched the moon, waiting for whatever was going to happen to happen, just wishing it was over, one way or the other.

A hot knife seemed to stab into his back, right between the shoulder blades, forcing him to arch his back while every joint seemed to come apart. This was worse than the other attacks, and his abused body could not even scream its misery. He lost complete control of his movements as bones were wrenched apart, flesh abused. He began to shake uncontrollably, and he finally admitted to himself that he was a failed, that he was going to die. The admission came with a sense of relief. At least the agony would be over.

Unexpectedly, with an almost audible click, the pain fled as pieces of his body began to slide into place. He looked up at the moon, and it seemed to both shrink away and take on a different tint, as if in an old black-and-white movie. He felt another fleeting wave of nausea, of disorientation, then surprisingly, a sense of calm. For a moment he wondered if he had died, but then he realized that he had made it. His first shift. He was a full-fledged member of the tribe.

Elation filled him where despair had taken over. What was he? What form was his?

The Pit seemed much bigger than it was when he had been shoved through the small door. He shook his head. The Pit was not important now. He tried to look down at himself, and saw fur. Well, with his family tree, that was to be expected. But just what was he? His vision, while a bit blurry, seemed to encompass everything around him all at once and without having to turn his head, and it was taking him a moment to get his bearings to make sense of what he was seeing. He brain was able to take in his new tail behind him. A naked, hairless tail.

Horror struck Rafe as he recognized that tail, what kind of animal had that tail. The blow was almost as bad as the pain of shifting. Rafe, to his despair, was a rat!

Part 1

Chapter 1
10 hours earlier

The afternoon before his First Shift, Rafe walked into the kitchen, dropping his school books on a chair and looking at what was for dinner. He lifted the lid off a pot on the stove only to have Jaira, the family's maid, smack his hand with a wooden spoon.

"You get out of there. You'll eat when the rest eat, and no sooner!" she admonished him in mock anger.

Rafe smiled and walked on, snatching a piece of cucumber that Jaira had been cutting on the counter. "Love you too, Jaira!"

He continued walking out into the family room. Well, it was designed as a family room, but his mom had commandeered it for her office. The huge wooden table-type desk took up most of the room, leaving a small tan couch under the window as the only other piece of furniture. His mom was on the computer as Rafe flopped down on the couch.

Without taking her eyes off the screen, she asked "Have a good day, dear?"

"Sure, mom. We got to eat human fetuses in biology, and then Mr. Sandusky and Miss Thierry acted out on the desk what we were taught in sex ed."

"That's good, honey."

Rafe snorted in amusement. "And now, Erica is coming over tonight so we can do our practical application homework on that."

"OK, have fun," she responded, fingers never slacking their assault on the keyboard.

Rafe looked at his mom with affection. She was a bit scatterbrained at times, but she was still a powerful figure in the tribe. Her black hair and slightly exotic looks were probably what got her quite a bit of attention in the jello world, but in the tribe, as a tiger, she was unusual and admired. Rafe didn't know of another tiger in the US, although he knew that they were not quite as rare in some Asian tribes. The why of that was beyond Rafe as he had not had his First Shift yet and so was not privy to the ways of the tribe, but he figured that as his mom was half Korean, that might have something to do with it.

Rafe wondered what his form would be, whenever that time came. His father was a wolf, which was no real surprise considering that over half of the tribe were wolves. But his dad was a pretty powerful wolf, so with a tiger as a mom, Rafe figured that he would be something powerful as well. Pre-shifters were kept on the dark about most things were, but Rafe seemed to be pretty popular with the female pre-shifters as if they knew his were-form would one day make him a powerful player within the tribe.

His mom took her tribal duties seriously. His father worked out in the world, the only were in a company of jellos. Were or not, money had to be earned, a living made. But that freed his mother up for tribal duties. Rafe still didn't know quite what those duties were as he was still a pre-shifter, but soon, he hoped, that would change. Five kids from his age group had already shifted, and Rafe was a little envious of their new status.

Rafe got up off the couch and left to go up to his room to do his homework before dinner. He gave his mom a squeeze on the shoulder as he walked past and went into the living room. This room was the only part of the house given over to the Korean part of the family. Korean furniture and art dominated the room, and there on her rosewood chair, his grandmother stood sentinel as was her wont.

"Hi, Gammy," Rafe said as he passed her.

A wizened hand reached out to grab him. Rafe was shocked as his grandmother was never too physically demonstrative.

She pulled him in with a surprisingly strong grip and buried her nose into his armpit. Rafe didn't know what to do. This was pretty weird. He wanted to pull back, but despite his size, he wasn't sure he would be able to do so.

She pulled her head back and stared at him for a moment before a smile creased her lips.

"Ann, Ann!" she called out. There was no response from his mom, so she stood up and went back into the family room, hand still clamped on Rafe's arm, dragging him along.

"Ann!" she called out once more, her slight Korean accent softening the "A" in his mom's name.

His mom held up a hand, finished typing, then looked up. "OK, *Omani*, what is—" she stopped as she saw the look in her mother's eyes and at Rafe in tow. Realization dawned on her.

"Are you sure?"

"I smell it. Now is his time for sure," Rafe's gammy told her with conviction.

Rafe's mom clasped her hands to her mouth, eyes shining, as it dawned on him just what his grandmother was saying. A sense of excitement crept over him. His First Shift? Today?

His mother stepped over to take Rafe in her arms and crush him to her. "Ah, my Rafe, tonight's the night. I'm so happy," she whispered into his ear.

Rafe felt a sense of euphoria. The time was finally upon him. He would be an adult. There was a small sense of dread as well. What if he was a failed? What if he was banished from the tribe? He couldn't take that. Or worse, what if the shift didn't complete? There were rumors told by the young ones to each other of grotesquely half-shifted weres, weres who died or were even killed. Could that be possible? Rafe pushed those thoughts down and buried them. His mother and father were both powerful weres. His older sister was also a strong, impressive wolf. It was in his genes, right?

The next eight or nine hours were a jumble of emotions and feelings. His father came home immediately after his mother called him. Other friends and relatives came by and mostly sat silently, only giving him a word of encouragement as they left.

He thought he wouldn't be thinking of food, but his stomach evidently didn't get the message that he should not eat before his First Shift. It rumbled menacingly, which turned Rafe's thoughts to his missed dinner. He was surprised that routine life could go on before such a momentous occasion.

Time seemed to crawl as they waited for moonrise, but at the same time, when moonrise did occur, it seemed to Rafe that no time had passed at all. He felt he needed a bit more time to mentally prepare himself.

The doorbell rang, and his father answered the door.

"Is this the home of one who is ready to evolve, one who is ready to take his part in the tribe and our race?" a voice intoned, the robed speaker covered by a hood.

The voice sounded familiar, but muffled by the hood, Rafe couldn't quite place who it was.

"Yes, it is," his father solemnly replied.

"Bring him to me," the voice ordered.

His mother took Rafe by the hand and brought him forward. Rafe looked back into the house, the last time he would be home as a child. He turned back and followed the hooded and robed figure. A good portion of the rest of the tribe followed in trace as the two walked down the street, over the baseball diamond, and to the back of the community center. Two more hooded people waited for them there. Rafe could feel something begin to build inside of him, something he couldn't quite place. He had time to look up at the rising moon before, without a word, the four of them entered the building. The others followed them inside and into the main meeting room, where Rafe and his escorts left them and went through the back offices and to the door leading to the vault. The vault was secured with a huge lock, the kind you see in the movies at a bank. One person spun it back and forth until it clicked, and the door ponderously opened. The vault was a mystery to the pre-shifters, but Rafe peered inside to see a normal-looking stairwell leading down. He followed the first person and was followed in turn by the other two. At the bottom of the stairs was a dimly lit passage. An emergency exit light seemed incongruous in this place, but building codes were building codes, Rafe guessed. Rafe followed his guide down the passage to the curved wall of the Pit. The existence of the Pit was no secret to the pre-shifters, nor to any jellos who came into the tribe's development. The round top was clearly visible in the trees in back of the community center. But Rafe had no idea of what was inside.

A small door, perhaps three feet high, blocked access to the Pit. The lead guide, turned around at the door. "Please remove your clothes."

Rafe had been told that he would go into the Pit naked. It didn't make much sense to shift and destroy whatever clothes he had, and he understood the symbolism of going into his second birth just as he came into the world from his first birth. But still, he felt uncomfortable taking his clothes off.

Once he was naked, the guide merely opened the door and stood aside and Rafe got on his hands and knees and crawled through. He was surprised at the austere nature of the Pit, and surprised that there was no roof, only a grating between the pit and the open sky. He shivered and crawled to the Pit's far wall, conscious that he was being observed. Well, he wasn't going to show fear, that was for sure. He sat down and waited for what was to come.

Chapter 2
after his shift

He wasn't sure how long he stayed in his rat form after his shift. Time didn't seem to be that important. Once, the door opened and one of the hooded men crawled through to stand silently and look at him. Rafe scurried to the far side of the Pit and looked up at him, fearful. Was that his very human fear of what the others would think, or was part of his rat core? The man stood there for a few moments before turning and crawling back out the door.

The moon made its way across the top of the Pit, and sometime after it had passed, Rafe felt a tugging, a pulling inside of him. It was if tenterhooks had latched onto his very essence, yanking him back. With much less pain, and in only a few moments, the human Rafe was back. Immediately, the door opened again, and two men came in, one handing him his clothes.

"Welcome, brother, into the tribe," was all one said as Rafe got dressed. Without a backwards glance Rafe followed them out of the Pit and down the passage into the community center.

The rec room was full of tribe members, most with forced smiles on their faces. A ragged round of applause broke out while his mom, dad, and two sisters came up to hug him.

"I'm so proud of you," his mom told him.

"But I'm a, I'm a...."

His mom put her finger up to his lips. "You are a were, a shapeshifter. A member of the tribe. You did not fail, and you are one of us."

"But a rat?" The despair surfaced in his plaintive croak.

"The Compact only states that a person must successfully shift and then shift back. Period," his dad interjected.

"But—"

"No buts. You'll learn more later." He tilted his head indicating Tabitha, Rafe's little sister, standing alongside of them and obviously confused.

"Your dad is right," his mom said. "Let's just enjoy the welcome. All of these people have been waiting here for you, so get some cake, walk about, and shake hands. You're still a Turner, and that means something to the tribe."

A table had been set up with a cake and a punchbowl. Besides the table was cooler filled with ice and cans of soda and beer. Rafe let himself be guided over where Mrs. St. John, evidently the mistress of the cake, offered him a piece.

"Here you go, young sir. Welcome to the tribe." Her hand touched his as she handed over the plate, and she brought her hand down and unconsciously wiped it on her red and white-checked apron. At least Rafe hoped it was unconsciously. It wasn't as if his "ratness" could change her own wolf shift-form. He was desperately hungry, though, so he wolfed down the cake. The "wolfing" aspect of that made him cringe, though.

The next half-an-hour was torture. He almost wished he was back in the Pit. No one made any mention of his shift-form at all, which was odd in-and-of-itself. When others made their First Shift, their form was usually mentioned, often trumpeted. Only Trevor seemed to make any reference to it. Trevor had done his First Shift only the month before, and he was a wolf, as was most of the tribe. He stood to the side with a Mountain Dew in his hand, and when he caught Rafe's eye, he wrinkled his nose up and down, then mimicked a rat using his paws to clean off his face. A day earlier, Rafe probably would not have taken any guff from Trevor. But now, he simply turned to his mother and told her he had to leave.

He walked out of the community center and made the walk home alone. Climbing the stairs up to his room, he didn't bother with the light or with his clothes. He simply lay down, pulled the blankets over him, and thought about his fate.

Chapter 3
later that afternoon

Rafe lay on the bed, face to the wall, pretending to be asleep. His mother sat next to him, fingers softly twirling his hair. She had been sitting there for about 20 minutes, and after an initial whispered "Rafe?" she had been silent. He just wished she would leave.

Finally, with a sigh, she got up and left, closing the door behind her.

"How is he?" his father asked her out in the hallway, their voices clear to him despite their subdued volume.

"He's not moving. I guess he's pretty disappointed."

"Of course he is. I just wonder what happened? A rat? There's nothing like that in either of our families."

"Who knows? Recessives work in mysterious ways. But he's healthy, and he made the shift. That's what matters," she responded.

"Yes, he's healthy all right. He's part of the tribe. But is it worth it?"

Rafe had been thinking the same thing, and tears started to well up in his eyes as his mother's voice raised an octave.

"Don't you even think that! Would you rather have him make a partial shift. Or what about Becky Throndson? Would you want that? A feral? Could you really go into the Pit and do what Jack had to do to her, his own daughter?"

"No, no, of course not! I don't mean that," he protested. "I just meant if he was a failed, and he could live a normal life out there."

"Well, it doesn't matter. He's a legal member of the tribe now. Rat or wolf or tiger, it doesn't matter. David Marten does fine for himself, right?" she asked.

"Sure, but he's respected, and the Manitoba Tribe has always been a bit touchy-feely, if you ask me."

"Maybe, but David wasn't always the 'wise elder.' He is what he is now because of what he has done with his life. Rafe can do the same."

His father's voice became a bit muffled, so Rafe didn't quite hear what he had to say, but his Grandmother's voice came through the door loud and clear.

"He rat. Bad luck for everybody. Bad face for family. You don't follow tradition, this happen."

"*Omani*! Quiet! He'll hear you!" his mother came back.

"No matter. He know it. He rat. No good for us."

Rafe did know it, and that is what hurt. He wasn't sure how he was going to face the tribe, how he was going to face his classmates. Maybe it would have been better had he become a failed. Better being a jello than a rat.

The door opened with a soft creak. He stiffened, wondering if his mother was coming back in. But his bed barely registered as a small form crept in and snuggled up against his back. Tiny arms tried to encircle his chest. He knew Tabitha had come to comfort him, not knowing why he needed it, though. A smile cracked his face, and he relaxed. For the first times since he got into bed hours before, he actually did fall asleep.

Chapter 4
4 weeks later

Rafe swore he would never shift again. A few tribe members never shifted, as far as he knew, so if he never did, maybe people would forget him and move on. After his reception at school, he wasn't sure anyone would forget, though.

The tribal school looked like a normal school, and it was certified by the state board of education, but it was strictly for children of tribe members. Children were kept in the dark about aspects of the were life, but they couldn't be living in the midst of shapeshifters and not absorb enough that innocent comments made to jello kids could have drastic consequences. So children were kept somewhat sequestered and on a short leash. It wasn't until after they completed their Revelations that they could go out into the world on their own.

Revelations for the latest group of shifters was scheduled to begin that weekend, but those who had had their First Shift already felt superior to the other kids. And a new hierarchy had begun to form. Rafe was mired at the very bottom. Throughout his growing up, Rafe had held a degree of alpha status. Bigger than the rest of the boys, and from one of the premier families in the tribe, others within his age group and younger tended to defer to him.

But not anymore. Trevor has assumed his spot, and Erica seemed to immediately shift her attention to the new top dog. It was bad enough that Trevor would make squeaking sounds when Rafe walked by, but even the younger kids got into the act. Rafe wanted to lash out, but he held back.

So Rafe wanted to fade into the background. He thought that never shifting again could achieve that. But as the moon became more and more full, Rafe felt a tug, an undefined need.

Rafe wasn't stupid. He could figure it out. And despite his depression, he wondered what it would be like to be a rat, to see the world through different eyes.

He had been warned not to shift unattended until after his Revelations, but he was damned if he was going to tell anyone that he needed to shift. And he was not going to give Trevor any more ammunition.

With the other tribe members who wanted to shift tonight probably going to the Ranch, the huge expanse of forest and fields behind the tribe's housing development, Rafe knew he had to go somewhere else. That left the jello world. He felt a twinge of guilt about that, but he figured that no one out there would blink an eye if he saw a rat. It was not like there would be a wolf or bear walking about in town, after all.

After dinner, Rafe told his mother and father that he didn't feel like watching tv, and that he was going to bed. They watched him walk up the stairs with concern, knowing that the first full moon after his First Shift was bringing back bad memories. His father started to get up to follow him, but his mother put her hand on his arm and told him to let Rafe go.

Rafe entered his room, then locked the door, listening for a moment to see if anyone was following him. He got out of his street clothes on put on a pair of shorts and a t-shirt. Opening his bedroom window, he looked down. It looked like a pretty long drop. In his sixteen years, he had never snuck out of the house, and he wondered if he could do it. For a moment, he contemplated letting the change sweep over him right then-and-there. A rat could probably make the climb easier. But he didn't want to try and change inside the tribe's territory.

He turned around and started to let himself out the window, legs first. He edged over further and further until he was only being supported by his lower arms, elbows, and hands which anchored him to the ledge. He figured his feet must be about ten feet above the ground. Taking a deep breath, he consigned himself to the fall and pushed off.

The landing was pretty anticlimactic. He fell back on his butt, but there was no pain, no discomfort. He shrugged and stood up, feeling fine. He glanced inside the windows on the side of the front door, but there was no movement. No one had heard him fall.

Feeling sure he would be caught, he started running, just a late-evening jogger out to increase his fitness level. A car passed him without incident, and he saw three people in the distance walking over in the direction of the gate to the Ranch, but no one paid any attention to him.

The security post for the development was unmanned, as it normally was at this hour of the evening. Rafe looked around to see if anyone was watching, then ducked under the gate and jogged off.

He had been in jello-land before, of course. But always with a full tribe member, always chaperoned. He could not suppress the shiver which went up his back. He had to chuckle at that. To the jellos, he was the boogeyman. Well, maybe not specifically him, but werewolves and the like were creatures of nightmares and horror. Yet here he was the one who was nervous.

He jogged on, looking for a likely place. Around their gated community, the jello houses were in other large developments, all gated communities as well. But they quickly shifted to smaller track homes, none of which offered any privacy. He was working up a sweat, and that seemed to increase the pull of the moon, which was just now appearing over the horizon.

He passed block after block of homes, all looking alike. People were out and about. Twice he had to shift to the other side of the street as people were out walking their dogs. Only one dog took notice of him, though, barking and lunging at its leash. Its owner shouted an apology across the street while pulling back against the dog.

Another jogger passed him, hand raised in greeting, one like-minded man to another. Rafe waved back, feeling a little guilty as he wasn't really in the brotherhood of fitness freaks.

The houses became a little smaller with smaller yards, most enclosed with chain link fences. His attention was caught by the glimpse of the traffic light on the main road ahead when something erupted at his feet, almost making his heart stop. He jumped off the sidewalk and into to the street before looking back. A small fluff of white, some sort of foo-foo dog, was jumping at the fence, trying desperately to get at Rafe, to destroy him. It barked furiously, jumping up and down. Rafe gave a nervous laugh before gathering himself and starting off again. The little dog paced, barking the entire time until it came up to the side fence, unable to chase Rafe any further. Rafe could hear the barking fade away as he continued on his way.

He finally came up against the main road, out of the housing area. The traffic light was green, so he ran across the road to the other side. He mentally flipped a coin before turning left and jogging on.

Running past the McDonalds on the corner, his stomach growled. He had been extremely hungry after his First Shift, so he thought he should have eaten more dinner. But he remembered vomiting as well, and he didn't want to give a rebellious stomach any ammunition. So he had barely touched his dinner at home.

The McDonalds was way too busy, so he jogged on. After another couple of hundred yards, he reached a small strip mall. All the stores were closed, even the small Mexican take-out place. It seemed early for a restaurant to close, but Rafe didn't know if it was primarily a lunch place or not. Even though they were not far from the tribe's home, Rafe, as a pre-shifter, had rarely gotten out in the area.

He slowed to a walk. The place looked deserted. Cars were whizzing by, and he didn't want to be too obvious, so he reached the end of the mall and quickly went around the corner and in back of it. A high concrete wall separated the mall from what looked to be storage lockers in the adjoining lot. About 5 yards separated the back wall of the mall buildings and the surrounding wall. Several dumpsters took position in this back passage, waiting to be emptied. This place looked perfect to him, or at least as perfect as he could expect.

He went past one dumpster and sat down on the other side, using its bulk as a shield. The overripe smell of "pre-rot" filled his senses. It bordered on the unpleasant, but it somehow gave him a feeling of comfort, of earthiness.

Sitting in the passage between the building and the wall, he knew he had to wait awhile until the moon was high enough to make itself seen. As he waited, his thoughts went back to his First Shift. His body seemed full of something, a yearning to do something, but he also remembered the searing agony of the change. His older sister had assured him that subsequent shifts were nothing like that, but still, he felt a degree of dread which warred with his need to shift.

After an eon or so, the moon finally peaked above the mall's rooftop. Rafe was in the shadow of the dumpster, so he shifted a bit into the direct moonlight, immediately feeling its siren call. Although he had not started his Revelations yet, kids always conferred on what they knew (or thought they knew), and Rafe understood that in order to shift, he had to clear his mind and will it to happen.

He closed his eyes and let the moonlight call him. He tried not to think of anything else, but the more he tried not to think of anything, the more he thought of things, all sorts of things. The sound of the cars driving by on the road at the front side of the mall, the feel of the concrete under him, the smell of the dumpster, all took a prime place in his thoughts at different times. And even though something inside of him cried out for release, he could not seem to grant it. Take a need to burp, the growing pressure inside, but nothing happening, and then multiply that by ten. That was how Rafe felt.

He sat up and shook his head. Looking up at the moon, he silently beseeched, *Help me, Mother Moon.*

The moon didn't move, didn't shimmer. But Rafe felt a renewed determination. He lay back down and tried to empty his mind of all except the need to shift. Nothing happened for a few moments, but maybe his prayer had been answered. He felt a twinge deep within himself, and with a cry, grasped at it. Which of course broke the connection, and everything stopped.

He calmed himself once again, thinking of nothing but the rat inside of him. When he felt the next subtle twinge, he didn't move, didn't make a sound. A second twinge followed, but with it came a faint but sharp stabbing pain. That frightened him. Claire had told him that only the First Shift was like that, only the First Shift had that unbearable pain. But what if she was wrong? Rafe sat up again.

The yearning was still inside of him, but now, the nervousness and fear were growing stronger. Memories of his body being torn apart invaded every aspect of his conscious thoughts. And that pretty much sealed the deal. For the next few hours, Rafe alternated between just sitting, gathering his courage, and lying down, trying to make the shift. The few times he felt any type of change, his fear surfaced, driving the rat back into his very depths.

The moon had long passed out of sight, and dawn was making its hesitant approach known when he wearily gave up. He trudged back to the tribe's compound, a yearning still inside, but defeat taking over him. At his house, he didn't even bother trying to find a surreptitious way back into his room. He merely opened the door and made his way up the stairs, never noticing his father sitting in the dark front room, watching his son with loving concern.

Chapter 5
first day of Revelations

Rafe entered the community center's classroom and moved to the back, ignoring the squeaking sound made by Trevor and the laughter of the others. He chose a free seat and sat down. It looked like he was the last one to arrive.

Trevor was there, of course, as was his joined-at-the-hip running mate, Jorge Martinez. Jorge was the only bear in the class. Erica was there, and it was not surprising that she was a wolf--a very attractive wolf, as wolves go, at least from what he had heard.

Sitting in the front row was Lief Kramer. Lief was the first one of their age group to have his First Shift. He was a coyote, a somewhat uncommon form, and if he thought that put him in a lower status than some of the others, he never let on. The others didn't seem to treat him any differently, and Rafe admired his attitude, even if that made him somewhat jealous. But there was a huge difference between a coyote and a rat, he knew.

The other wolves were there: both Robs (Goodpaster and Smith), Andy Filipović, Kat Kean, and Jenifer (one "n," not two, as she reminded everyone). And then there was Alysha Moore. Alysha was the last one to reach First Shift, which she achieved the day after Rafe's ill-fated attempt to shift on his own. First Shifts generally were easier on the exact date of the full moon, but they often happened a few days on either side of it.

Alysha was a golden eagle. Raptors were somewhat rare, and there hadn't been another eagle in the tribe in anyone's memory, although there were two hawks. Alysha would take part in Revelations with the rest of them, but she would go join the Ft. Collins tribe every other weekend for some more specific ornithological training.

Jonathan P. Brazee

The door opened, and Mr. Peterson shuffled in. Wearing his ever-present olive-green sweater, with his hunched shoulders and shock of white hair, he was a familiar sight within the tribe. All the tribe members who had gone through their First Shift within the last 45 years had received their Revelations from him.

Everyone shifted their attention to him as he got to the podium. He slowly looked at the class, seemingly appraising each one of them. "Welcome, tribe members," he finally said in a soft but firm voice.

"I am Mr. Peterson," he told them, as if each one of them didn't know exactly who he was. "For the next three months, you will spend each afternoon after school with me, each weekend with me. I will endeavor to teach you what it means to be a member of our tribe, of our race. I will try to teach you how to make best use of your gifts."

He paused and seemed to change tack. "Why is it that it is only now that we begin to teach?" No one responded. "This is not a rhetorical question. Mr. Smith," he pointed to Rob. "Why don't we teach you anything about being a were, a shifter, until after your First Shift?"

Rob looked a little uncomfortable. All of them had wondered that at some time or another. It was difficult living in a community of weres but not knowing anything about them.

"Mmm, because we wouldn't understand anything yet?"

"Did you have your sex ed classes in the mainline school? Had any of you had sex before that? And no, that was a rhetorical question. I don't need to know who of you are still virgins."

The class broke out in embarrassed laughter.

"The reason we keep the young ones in the dark is simple. We must protect our race. And that is the prime directive that each of you needs to embrace." He paused again. "What happens if you fail in your First Shift? What happened to Maggie Clark last December?"

"She failed, and so she was sent out to the rest of the jellos," Trevor quickly offered.

"'Jellos.' Yes, well, I will get to that later. But yes, she was given a new start outside of the tribe. Do you know what used to happen to those who failed? Even here in our tribe, only as far back as your grandparents? Back when I had my First Shift? They were killed," he said bluntly.

There was a collective gasp from the class. Oh, there were whispered rumors, the same as stories about ghosts, vampires, and things which go bump in the night. But some things were never mentioned aloud to the grownups. Some things were taboo. And now, Mr. Peterson was openly telling them that this was more than a way to scare young kids. This was a fact.

"Make no doubt about it. We have enemies out there in the Static world. We've been the target of genocide more times than we can count. And so our defense is secrecy. We may be stronger than them, we may heal faster, but our non-shifting brethren will always be more numerous. There will always be more to take their places."

Most of the students were shifting uncomfortably in their seats.

"We killed those who failed to shift so they could not betray us," he continued. "So they could not go into the other world, upset at not being one of us, ready to take revenge. Some tribes still do that even today. Mr. Turner, your grandmother is from Korea, correct?"

Rafe sunk down into his seat as the others turned to look at him. "Ye. . .yes, sir," he stammered.

"Well, they still kill their failed shifters there, today. They do that in many of the Asian tribes, the Middle-Eastern tribes, the East-European tribes. They did it in the Everglades tribe until about 10 years ago. We don't. We set them up with a new life on the outside. But when they go, they have no more knowledge of being a were than what you can see on television, what you can read in books. If they move against us, they can't give any vital information away."

The class was silent.

"But if we must kill, we will. Get used to the idea. It's not only those who fail who don't become part of the tribe. Sometimes, rarely, thank goodness, a person will partially shift, stopping in neither human nor animal form. Usually, this state in untenable, and the poor soul dies. But others shift too much, they go too far."

"Ferals," Kat interjected.

"Yes, ferals, Miss Kean. They have gone too far. They are wholly animal, and cannot shift back until they die, if then. And they are put down like rabid dogs."

They exchanged knowing glances to each other. The year before, Becky Throndson had gone into the Pit. One of the robed attendants had eventually come out and quietly spoken to Mr. Throndson, whose knees seemed to give out as he took in whatever was being said. He seemed to steel himself, and he followed the robed attendant back into the Pit. The gathering quickly broke up, and Becky was never seen again. Even the faileds were given a chance to say their goodbyes. No one ever mentioned Becky again, and this confirmed what they had surmised but were afraid to ask.

"A full grown wolf suddenly appearing in New York, in London, in Beijing, a wolf who kills, and more importantly, a wolf who might shift back to human form upon being killed, well, that would bring unwanted and unacceptable attention to us. It has to be done."

"That is why the Pit has grating on top, in case a feral is a raptor. And why the door is so small. Unless you can crawl out in your human form, you are not getting out again alive."

He took a moment to survey their faces, to take in their reaction. "And that is enough for our first lesson. I don't want to dilute the message. The tribe must survive. Sear that into your hearts."

His mood lightened up. "And no homework for today, so enjoy the freedom." He picked up a brown paper bag which was on the table in front of the classroom. "OK, all of you come up and get your tribe medallions."

That rather surprised Rafe. The medallion was what showed others that you belonged, that you were a member of your tribe. Not all of the older people wore them all the time, but most of the younger did. Rafe thought there would be some sort of ceremony in giving them out. Just reaching in a ratty paper bag and pulling out a medallion packaged in clear plastic seemed somewhat routine.

He opened up the small plastic bag and held out the medallion. It was a little thicker than it looked at first glance, but his attention was on image of the three pine trees, the tribe's symbol. This marked him as a full member of the tribe, and any other were seeing this would know him for that.

"Same time tomorrow afternoon, class. And be ready for some real lessons. Bring your medallions."

He slipped the medallion over his neck and walked home.

Chapter 6

Rafe walked through the front door and into the kitchen. Jaira was cooking as normal, and he performed his usual of pulling off lids to look what was for supper. Jaira did her equally usual slapping at his hands with a wooden spoon.

"Love you, Jaira!" he called out in passing, going in to see his mother. She was busy at her computer, so he merely leaned in and gave her a peck on the cheek.

"How was school?" she asked absently. Then catching herself, she stopped typing and looked up. "I mean, how was Revelations class?"

She reached out and pulled his medallion away from his body a bit so she could see it, and with a smile, let it drop back on his chest.

"Interesting, I should say. At the least."

"You need to talk about it?"

He shrugged. "No. Why should I?"

"Well, honey, if you ever do have questions, you can always ask your dad or me. Or your sister."

"Yeah, no problem." He walked out into the front room and plopped himself on the couch. His grandmother was sitting on her chair, but when he came in, she got up, muttering about bad luck, and made a warding sign towards him before walking out. Rafe was getting rather tired of her attitude, to be honest.

He picked up the remote and started flipping through the channels, settling on FoodTV. Sometimes he liked to watch what Ramsay or Batali were preparing when at the same time, he could smell Jaira's cooking. He bet Jaira could give them a run for their money.

Tabitha came rushing into the room. "Rafe!" She jumped on the couch and snuggled half of her body into his lap.

"Hey Tabby Cat!"

"I'm not a cat! I don't know what I'll be yet." This was a ritual between them.

"But you will always be my Tabby Cat," he said as he put his arm around her.

"Meow," she replied with her little girl giggle.

They watched the amateur chefs on the television show trying to outdo each other in order to win their own restaurant. Rafe couldn't cook himself, but he liked watching these shows. After awhile, he felt a bit of wetness, and looked down to see Tabith had fallen asleep, a thin line of drool coming out of her mouth and now collecting on his shirt. He just smiled. No matter what his form was, he could count on his Tabby Cat to love him.

"She really adores you, you know?"

He hadn't seen Claire walk in. She had a way of moving that was graceful and animalistic, even when she was in human form. She sat down in Gammy's chair and looked at him.

"Yeah, I know. My Tabby Cat."

"How come you never looked up to me like that, little bro?" she asked with a smile.

"Ah, you kept yelling at me to leave you alone, to get out of your room," he said with a laugh.

"Maybe so, maybe so," she laughed with him. She got a little more serious. "How're you doing?"

He knew what she was really asking, but he didn't want to go there yet. "I'm fine. No problems."

"You know, I'm here for you." She looked concerned.

While Rafe wished his grandmother would get off his case, he wished the rest of his family would quit walking on eggshells around him. It was what it was. He was just going to have to deal with it.

He looked up at his sister. Really looked. To him, she would always be that slightly gawky older sister, playing with Barbie dolls one moment, out playing soccer with the boys the next. But looking at her, he realized what a beauty she had become. There were various standards of beauty in their animal forms, but perceived beauty in one form was not an indication of beauty in another form. Claire, though, had it all. She was stunning as a young woman, a true heart-breaker. But now that Rafe had seen her more fully in her wolf form, he had to admit that she was one good-looking wolf. Coupled with their family prestige (if Rafe hadn't ruined that, he thought ruefully), she was the penultimate "catch" for some lucky guy. She did favor one guy in particular, but it wasn't as if she didn't have a lot of choices.

"Yeah, I know."

There was an awkward bit of silence before Claire broke it. She slapped both hands on her knees and got up. "Well, I'm off to see Rhett!"

"Frankly, my dear, I don't give a damn," he told her.

"You know, that wasn't funny the first hundred times you've said that. And it won't be funny the next hundred times."

"I guess I just have to work on my delivery, 'cause that's funny!"

"Yeah, right!" She gave him a squeeze on his shoulder as she walked by.

He reached out and grabbed her arm. "Claire?"

She looked down at him, a question in her eyes.

"What's it like? I mean, with Rhett?"

"Rhett? You know him. He's funny, and he treats me like a lady. I can talk with him."

"No. I mean. . .I mean, you know, running."

"Ah," was all she said for a moment. She sat down beside him, careful not to disturb the sleeping Tabitha. "It's, it's. . ." She stopped. "It's like. . ." She stopped again. She took a breath. "I can't describe it. When I'm with Rhett, he is so polite, so kind. But after we shift, it's like we both change. I mean, I'm still me, and he's still him. But now, we can smell each other, we can smell everything. The whole world gets deeper, more intense. And so we run. Side by side we run. That makes the smells stronger, like they're being jammed into our noses. And I feel his movements, even before he makes them, if that makes sense. It is like we're tied together. And he's such a, a, such an animal!"

She sat still for another moment. "I feel like there are no problems in the world. And I know Rhett is my other half. I get a little let down when we shift back, to be honest," she told him, her voice a bit more subdued. "But you'll see! When you find someone to run—" She pulled back, hand to her mouth in horror.

Rafe shook his head slightly. He reached over and pulled Claire's hand down from over her mouth. "It's OK. I know better than anyone what my chances are to find someone to run with. Don't worry."

"I'm so sorry!"

"It's OK. Really, it is." But it wasn't.

Chapter 7
back in class

"So we don't need the moon? I don't understand." Rob G had proven to be the slowest to grasp things in the class, and this time was no different.

Mr. Peterson seemed to struggle to suppress a sigh. "That is what I have been trying to tell you. The ability to shift is inside of you, not outside."

"But why do I feel the pull when the moon is full?"

"Part of it is the placebo effect. You know the moon is full, and that puts you in the right frame of mind. But yes, the moon does have its own effect as well on us. And that is one reason most of our recreational shifting, shall we call it, is done around the full moon." He turned his attention away from Rob. "But I'll go over it again. You know now that we have a gene which makes us different than other people, a gene that allows us to shift. That's what I mean when I tell you that the ability to shift is inside of you. But what was the hormone I told you?"

"Lycanmone. . .lyca. . ." the class murmured, then fell silent.

"*Lycantonin!*" he reminded them with perhaps a little more exasperation that he intended to show. "And what's the albedo of the moon?"

"Zero-point-one-three-six," the rest of the class intoned.

"Well, you remembered something, at least, from a whole. . ." he glanced at his watch, "five minutes ago. It is at this strength and spectrum where our bodies are excited into producing the lycantonin, and it's lycantonin that facilitates shifting." He looked for something, anything to dawn in Rob's eyes.

"So we need the moon to produce the lycan. . .lycantonin?" Kat asked.

"No, it's already in your body. After you reach puberty, that is. And that is the trigger which makes us what we are. OK, let me put this another way." He started pacing in front of the room. "You all know what melatonin is." There was no response. "Come on class, let me see that you're alive. Melatonin?"

There were nods from most of the students.

"Melatonin is a hormone produced in the pineal gland. We all have it, 24 hours a day. Daylight, or I should say the blue light frequencies of daylight, inhibits the production of melatonin. And since it makes us sleepy, during the day, we have less when we need to be awake, but at night, without the blue light, more of it is produced, and we feel sleepy. But we can still sleep in the daylight, right? We don't need to take melatonin to sleep, right? It just makes it easier for us to sleep.

"Same for lycantonin. After puberty, your body starts producing it. Like with melatonin, with blue light, at about 470 nanometers, for anyone who is interested in that amount of detail, the production of lycantonin is affected. But yellow light tends to decrease it, and the yellow light seems to be stronger in its effect. Since moonlight is mostly blue light with yellow light filtered out due to the albedo properties of the moon's surface, moonlight, well, under the full moon, that's when your body will produce the highest amount of lycantonin. That's why it's easier to shift, especially the first time, when the moon is full.

"And hence your tribal medallions. What are they for?"

"So people know what tribe we are. I mean, what tribe we belong to," answered Trevor.

"Partly, but not completely. Take your medallions off." There was a rustle as the students complied. "Now look at the top. See that little bump there? I want you to push that bump to the side, just slide it."

Rafe put his thumb on the bump and pushed. It slid, and as it hit a stop, a light came on from the back. The bluish light washed over his hands and arms, and surprisingly, he felt a tug from his inner rat, that twinge which wanted him to shift. There were assorted "oohs" and "aahs" from the rest of the class.

"Your medallions, my friends, are aids in shifting. The light coming from them has been calibrated to excite the maximum production of lycantonin. This will help you shift, even if there is no full moon. Turn them off now, though. We'll go over the lights in more detail after the break."

"But I know people can shift any time. My father does it, and he almost never wears his medallion," Kat pointed out. "How can they if it is bright sunlight? It doesn't make sense."

This time Mr. Peterson let the sigh out without bothering to suppress it. "As I have told you, shifting is inside of you. It's in the mind. I don't want to jump the gun here. You're asking about tomorrow's lesson. But to be brief, you have it in you to shift at any time. It just takes training. You will have many exercises with Ms. Baumgardner to master that."

"Ms. Baumgardner? The yoga lady?" asked Trevor.

"Yes, the 'yoga lady.' She has to make a living, after all. But her most important mission is to help new weres master their own minds. And, to be truthful, you do that rather like people do yoga."

"Let me ask you something. How many of you have tried to shift since your First Shift?" No hands were raised. "OK, OK. I know you were told not to try it alone, and I'm not going to turn you into the Shift Nazis." That raised a chuckle from the class.

"Let me re-phrase that. How many of you managed a shift on your own since your First Shift." Once again, no hands were raised. "Ah, now you are being honest. Mr. Kramer, let me ask you, how did your First Shift feel?"

"Feel? It hurt like hell!" he burst out.

"Aye, there's the rub." No one blinked an eye. "'Aye, there's the rub?' What, no comprehension? Shakespeare anyone?" He paused for a moment to take in the class' silence. "What are they teaching our youth nowadays?"

That last question did not really seem to be aimed at any of the students.

"Yes, First Shifts are agonizing. And that causes a problem. It's that memory of the pain which puts up a block to shifting again. Even if you want to shift again, it's that block which keeps you. All of us try to shift again. It's in our very nature. But it takes a long time and many sessions before you will be able to break through that mental block and shift once more. We can tell you and tell you until we're blue in the face, and you can even believe us, but your inner being won't believe us until you experience it."

Trevor began to ask something, but Mr. Peterson forestalled him with a raised hand. "Yes, even without your classes, you would eventually shift. The call is just too strong to resist, after all. But believe me, this will make your next shift happen much, much sooner.

"And my point is that your inability to shift now is strictly a mental block. And if your mind can keep you from shifting?"

"Your mind can control your shifting, make you shift," Alysha offered with a smile.

"Bingo, Miss Moore. You get a gold star for that!"

Rafe thought about that, about his attempt at shifting. It made sense. He wanted to shift. He needed to shift. But it was the fear, the fear of pain which stopped him each time he started to go into transition.

He looked up at Mr. Peterson, mind going blank as he waited for class to finish. He wanted try something.

Jonathan P. Brazee

Chapter 8
later that evening

Rafe sat down by the dumpster. He had been anxious to make this second attempt, but he also wanted all the stores in the strip mall to be closed. A few minutes before nine, with his medallion tucked inside his pocket, he casually sauntered out of the house and made his way out of the development, down to the highway, and in back of the mall.

He felt a rising sense of excitement. Could he do it? Mr. Peterson had said that it might take quite awhile to be able to shift again, but he had to find out. He had been so close before.

Leaning back beside the dumpster until he was supine, he closed his eyes and tried to ignore the clammy wetness soaking into his shirt, the more pronounced smell of garbage. Reaching into his pocket, he pulled out his medallion, turning it on before putting it under his shirt so the light was directly shining on his skin. Immediately, he felt the pull. Part of his mind wondered if the light could actually work so quickly, or if merely turning it on was part of the placebo effect Mr. Peterson had described, but he pushed that fleeting thought aside.

His hour on the internet researching yoga hadn't done him much good, but he tried to take what little he had learned and put it to use. Yoga seemed to focus around breathing, so he tried to take deeper, slower breaths. It seemed to calm him down a bit, but he realized that could just be wishful thinking.

As he calmed, he started thinking about the rat inside of him. He knew the rat was him, that he was the rat, but it helped to think of the rat as a separate being, one that wanted to come out but needed to be coaxed, needed to be convinced it was safe. In less time than Rafe would have imagined, he felt the rat stir. His heart rate jumped up a bit in excitement, so he concentrated on breathing. In and out. Slower. Deeper.

The yearning grew. He knew he could shift. He just needed it to break free. As he felt his sense of who he was stretch, he felt a shift begin. And immediately, the fear came back, driving his rat back into the recesses.

He sat up, gulping the air. Disappointment came over him. He had failed again. Why did he think he was any different? Why did he think he could make a shift alone? He thought about going home, but his perverse and often stubborn nature kept him sitting in the dirty alley. He steeled himself and lay back down. Almost by force of will alone, which didn't seem too yoga-like, from what he had read, he slowed his breathing.

Determination didn't always jive with being calm, but that was his mood. Unless everyone he knew was in on some huge joke, that every one of them was lying, he knew that his next shift would not be like his first. He knew it in his brain. He just had to convince his rat of that.

He silently summoned the rat. The rat stirred. His heart jumped a beat, but he pushed back on it, slowing it down again. The yearning increased again. Incongruously, his skin began to itch, but he spared that only a brief thought.

He pictured the rat poking his nose out, seeing if the coast was clear. *Come on out, boy! I know you want to*, he thought. Emboldened, the rat moved forward, then looked up, staring right into his mind, if that made sense. Rafe's eyes were closed, but it seemed as if his imagined rat was meeting his gaze.

He felt the shift building inside of him. On his First Shift, the agony had kept him from noticing much else. Now he could feel more of the experience. The rat in his mind's eye began to swell in size, filling his very being. Then there was a slight twinge of pain, and the panic made its appearance.

"No!" he shouted aloud. He was not going to be denied. As the rat turned to flee back to safety, he reached into himself and grabbed a nebulous, naked tail. With a concerted effort, he pulled with all his willpower, refusing to give into fear. And the rat came.

Chapter 9

Darkness surrounded Rafe, and something was pushing against him. He didn't know what was going on. Had he failed? A small sense of panic hit him and he tried to run, but it was like running through quicksand. Then his head popped through, and he felt a sense of relief. He had done it! The darkness? The pressure? That was his clothes. He had shifted and ended up inside his shirt. He hadn't thought of what would happen to his clothes. Well, this was one benefit of being smaller in his animal form. If he had turned into a bear or something, his clothes would not have survived.

Getting his bearings, he looked around. But maybe "looking around" was not the correct term. He could see all around him, but he wasn't moving his head. He realized that his scope of vision was essentially 360 degrees. It was freaky, and he wondered that his mind didn't break down, but things seemed to work.

His vision was fuzzy, though. Nothing seemed to be quite in focus. Did rats have weaker vision than humans?

He felt a little uncomfortable out in the open, so he scurried back behind the dumpster, which had taken on huge proportions. He lifted his nose and sniffed. What had been a single, rotting stench to his human nose suddenly took on a myriad of individual aromas, all swirling and dancing with each other. He could pick out the rot, still, but now it just didn't seem like a bad smell. The origin of other smells escaped him, but he was curious to find out just what they were.

Without thinking, he hopped up to the cross support of the dumpster, then with one more hop, he was at the lip, looking down at the bounty inside. His eyes picked up some florescent spotting along some of the garbage. His nose also seemed to hone in on those spots, as if he could pinpoint the location of any smell. From somewhere, he knew those spots were rat urine. Why they were florescent, and how he knew what they were was beyond him and something to contemplate later.

He jumped down onto the garbage, landing on a black plastic bag. The variety and strength of the aromas assaulting his nose was extraordinary. "Assaulting" his nose was probably too aggressive. Caressing? Enveloping? There was no discomfort about any of this.

He caught a familiar scent, one he recognized, and immediately turned in that direction and jumped. Pushing over a styrofoam lunch container, he uncovered an apple. He felt accomplishment that he recognized something in this aroma soup. How he had been able to pinpoint it, though, he wondered. He took a few tentative sniffs and realized that he was smelling through two separate nostrils, each one individually. It took some concentration, but he could discern a difference in the strength of a smell in each nostril, and that helped him locate the source of the smell. It was easier not to think about it, though, and just go with nature.

He wasn't sure just how long he spent exploring the dumpster. Where he would probably have been disgusted crawling through it in his human form, it now seemed like a natural and interesting thing to do. He even nibbled on a half-eaten tamale, but that was more of an experiment rather than trying to assuage his increasing hunger. And as with his sense of smell, the tamale took on a whole new spectrum of tastes and senses.

Eventually, he realized that he should be getting back. He was relishing the freedom, the barrage of senses he was experiencing. But he was still Rafe Turner, and he still had a geometry quiz in the morning. So with some reluctance, he hopped up to the dumpster's rim, then down to the ground.

His clothes were still lying on the ground next to the dumpster. He scurried on top of his shirt, then tried to relax. His could feel his rat heart beating much faster than his human heart beat, and to try and relax and slow that heartbeat down was difficult. Being out in the open also contributed to his stress.

His inner human did want to come out. He could feel it. But it just wasn't happening. He wondered if perhaps he needed his medallion. Pushing himself under his shirt collar, he made his way down inside his shirt until he came up against the medallion. The light was still on—he was glad he had been given a full-size medallion, unlike Alysha, who had been given a smaller, bird-only medallion. Mr. Peterson had said that Alysha's medallion had a much shorter battery life.

Under the light's glow, he could feel the pressure to change build, just as when he changed into his rat form. He crouched down, whiskers quivering in the charged atmosphere. Calming his mind, he called forth the human Rafe—and was suddenly being strangled.

He shouted out, flailing his arms. Fighting off his opponent, he pulled it off his neck and threw it on the ground. Puffing, he looked at it for a moment, before breaking out into loud laughter. Standing in a dirty alley, stark naked, he had bravely fought off his shirt. Next time, he promised himself, he would change back outside of his clothes rather than inside, and only then get dressed.

His stomach growled, making its empty situation known. He got dressed and walked back out in front of the strip mall and started back. Passing the McDonalds, his stomach protested even louder. He went through his pockets, and luckily, he had enough for a Big Mac meal.

The bored-looking and rather fat young lady taking his order never gave him a second glance. Rafe wondered what she would do if he changed right then and there. He figured all weres were sometimes tempted to show off, to go back to the era where they could awe and even terrorize jellos. His was only a passing thought, though.

Slamming down his Big Mac, fries, and coke only partially satisfied his hunger, but it would have to do as he didn't have enough money for anything else. There was nothing left to do but go home and see if Jaira might have put a little of the chicken pot pie they had for dinner in the fridge.

Rafe knew he was a full member of the tribe, even if his animal form was not very impressive. But now, that he had managed shifting a second time, something he was told he needed time and assistance to do, well, he felt much more comfortable in who he was, much more a real, full-fledged member. OK, he wasn't a wolf, a tiger like his mom, or even a coyote, and maybe a rat didn't seem like much, but tonight, he had felt good about himself, he felt fulfilled. And if others didn't like that, well, fuck 'em.

Chapter 10
back in class

As Mr. Peterson droned on, Rafe looked at the others in his class. Except for Alysha, who was having her own such classes with the Ft. Collins tribe, they had all spent the last two hours going through meditation and thought-focusing techniques with Ms. Baumgardner. Rafe had been tempted to tell her that he didn't need them, that he could already shift on his own, but he had already decided that discretion being the better part of valor, maybe he shouldn't be going around trumpeting any such skills now. The others would soon be able to shift as well, and then they would have their stronger, more exciting forms, while he would still be a rat.

Now, with Alysha joining them, they were back in class. He wondered if any of them had managed to shift on their own, yet. Looking at Trevor, he snorted in amusement picturing his reaction if he found out that he could shift.

"Something funny, Mr. Turner?"

Rafe snapped back to reality. "Oh, no sir. I was just thinking."

"Try not to strain your brain, then. I know that 'thinking, " he made quote marks with his fingers in the air while stressing the word, "is not that common an occurrence with you."

The rest of the class chuckled at Mr. Peterson's rejoinder.

"Well, to get back at what I was saying before Mr. Turner decided to 'think,' " the teacher said, once again making the finger quotation mark signs, "no one knows just when the first mutation which allowed shifting made its appearance. Nor where, for that matter. The earliest recorded histories, the earliest art, even back in paleolithic times, showed evidence that some people could shift. There are Turkish cave paintings from 8,000 BC which depict werewolves, and the Epic of Gilgamesh also refers to us. Certainly, we have been here a long time."

"Does anyone know why people seem to shift to animal forms native to their genetic heritage? Mr. Smith? Ms. Kean? Mr. Filipović? Anybody?"

No one even pretended to begin to respond.

"Well, that is sort of a trick question. No one really knows, and we have people in some of the best biotech companies now trying to decipher our genetic history via DNA analysis, although the companies don't really know that, of course. But if weres started in one corner of the world by a simple mutation, then shouldn't all modern weres be limited to shifting into a single form, or at least forms native to the original area? But as you all know, people of European ancestry tend to shift into primarily wolves, lynxes, and bears; Asians into bears, tigers, and leopards; Indians...oh sorry, I mean Native Americans, into wolves, bobcats, bears, and coyotes, and Africans into lions, jackals, hyenas, leopards, and cheetahs. Oh yeah, Australians almost all into either dingos or Tasmanian devils. I will talk a bit more on our raptor friends," he nodded at Alysha, " and selkies a bit later, but the point is that people change forms to those native to their genetic homeland."

"So what about Turner? His genetic homeland is the city dump?" Trevor asked with a laugh. The rest of the class laughed along, louder and with more feeling than when they laughed at Mr. Peterson's attempt at humor a few moments before.

"That's enough, Mr. Mueller. To get back on track. And because the shifting gene first made its appearance in our prehistory, we only shift into animals which were around then. Hence, none of us shift into dogs, which didn't make an appearance until after the first of us appeared. In fact, it may be that dogs were specifically bred as protection against us, as an identification tool, so-to-speak. This was especially true in what is now Europe. Most of us here have a European background, and we are perhaps the main reason that we have enemies out there, that we had to form the United Tribes."

"Australian and Native American weres tended to live more peacefully among their Static cousins. Some served as local shamans and were considered skilled in the ways of the gods. But the European weres, many of them looked upon other people as lesser beings."

"Yeah, jellos can't do what we do," added Trevor, looking around for another round of laughter.

" 'Jellos.' That lovely term. Mr. Mueller, do you know why some of you call other people 'jellos?' "

"'Cause they're, um, 'cause they're like jello?"

"And how are they like jello?"

"I don't know, they just are."

Mr. Peterson sighed before continuing. "In 1897, Pearl Waite invented a dessert which he named Jell-O. He sold it for $450 to Orator Frank Woodward in 1899, and by 1902, the product was a national name. And what is Jell-O? A tasty dessert which quivers and trembles. Which describes the prey of some of your great grandparents, of my own parents. Not the cows and sheep we have at the Ranch for you to prey upon, but people. Just like in the Middle Ages in Europe when weres routinely preyed upon people. And just like here in the good old USA, where some of our ancestors felt it their God-given right to prey on 'inferior' species, namely other people. People who tasted good and who trembled in fear when a werewolf came a'knocking. So think of that when you use that term. Think of sinking your teeth into the clerk of the 7-11 instead of one of their hotdogs."

The class was silent. Rafe actually gulped. He had never really thought of it that way. He knew, as all members of the tribe knew, that in the "olden days," weres did prey on other people. But now? They were more civilized now, right? He thought of the fat cashier at McDonalds, of eating her instead of a Big Mac, and his stomach turned. Right then and there, he vowed not to use the jello term again. "Statics" is what some others used, and that seemed innocent enough. Or just "people."

"Be absolutely sure of one thing. Humans who can shift and humans who can't are still the same species. We can interbreed with them, we can have children. Some can shift, even if most can't. Even two Static humans can have a baby capable of shifting, if the recessive genes align just right."

"And it is this tendency for our European branch of the family, especially wolves, to use other people as prey, which caused us to form the United Tribes. As other people gained in technology, as the wild habitat was cut down for cities and factories, there were fewer places to hide. We had to do something, so we formed the United Tribes, made a vow not to feed on people, and hunted down all the rogues who refused to comply with us."

"Some tribes are not as strongly connected with the rest, like the North Korean tribe, and there have been rumors that some isolated tribes revert every once in awhile, but generally, we do not hunt people, and we cooperate with each other for the benefit of us all. We still have enemies, and we will have an entire class on that on another day, but for now, we try to blend into society and live in harmony with the rest of the population."

Chapter 11
three weeks later

Rafe tried to slip out as often as he could over the next couple of weeks in order to shift. He didn't even take his medallion anymore. He could shift without it. As the moon became closer to full, it became easier, but he didn't need it. He never shifted on tribal land, afraid that someone else would pick up the scent and know he had done so.

In class with Ms. Baumgardner, he still played the slow learner. Everyone applauded Kat when she made her second shift, but Rafe had decided to wait until about half of the class had managed a shift before he shifted again in public. He didn't want to seem too good at it, but being too weak at it presented its own set of problems.

He finished his homework and slipped out, making sure he had enough money in his pocket for two value meals. Each time he shifted, he was famished, and he discovered that by eating before he shifted, he could cut down on that gnawing hunger.

Walking out of the development was routine now. As an adult, he could come and go as he pleased. It was a brisk 20 minute walk to the stoplight; but first, he had to pass the mad foo-foo dog. It seemed to be waiting for him and started barking as soon as he came into sight. Mr. Peterson had told the class that most animals seemed to be able to smell the lycantonin, and it drove some animals, especially some dogs, into either frenzy or abject fear. That explained why very few, if any, weres had pets other than fish.

As he reached Foo-foo's yard, the little dog was jumping up two or three times its height, telling the world to watch out for this dangerous creature walking amongst them. Rafe suddenly turned to the little dog and stamped his feet, yelling out, trying to startle it. The dog never stopped its tirade. He pointed a finger at it and nodded, having to admit that it was a brave little thing.

Rafe continued on, and as he reached and crossed the main road, he could feel the rat stir. He knew this was probably the Pavlovian Response he had studied in class, that the road marked a boundary to where he could shift, but he didn't care.

He almost bounced into Micky D's. "Hey Jenny, how's it going tonight?" The same bored- looking girl who served him on his first night out served him most nights, but now, she always perked up when Rafe arrived. He didn't even have to order.

"A Big Mac Meal, a Filet-O-Fish Meal, all upsized with one Mt. Dew and one Dr. Pepper."

"Ah, you know me well, Jenny!"

"Same thing every night you come. You've got to try our McRib sometimes, though. It's really good," she told him with a helpful smile.

"I'm a man who likes my routine," he said with a dramatically gruff voice.

She laughed. "Suit yourself."

Jenny was about his age, he figured, or maybe a bit older. He enjoyed their little give and take. Back with the tribe, he still felt unsure and withdrawn. This was in direct conflict of how he felt about himself now that he had been changing. He felt good each time he shifted. But back with the tribe, he felt inadequate. Being out here in Static-land, however, with people who could not change at all, well, that let him come out of his shell.

She took his money and gave him his change. There was writing on the receipt. When he looked at it, he realized it was a phone number. He quickly looked up at Jenny, and she had a nervous smile on her face. She gave a little shrug.

Jenny was probably not the kind of girl who had guys drooling after her. Rather overweight and with patches of pink skin on her face and neck, Rafe figured she had never been part of an in-crowd. And with what had been happening to him since his First Shift, he understood what it felt to be on the outside looking in. So he appreciated the courage it took for Jenny to make a move, to try for something she wanted.

As he took all of this in, he could see her hopeful look fade a bit, just one more rejection. He picked up the paper, gave it a kiss, and made a show of putting it in his wallet. He matched her growing smile, and with a nod, took a table to wolf down his meal.

The food was gone in moments, his rat making eager stirrings to emerge. He left, but not before tipping an imaginary hat to Jenny. She lifted her hand to her ear with thumb and little finger extended, the universal "call me" sign.

He hurried to his strip mall and went in back to El Ranchito's dumpster. He reminded himself that sometime he had to actually go there as a customer. Their food smelled good to his rat nose, and he felt he owed them something for use of their space.

Taking off his clothes, he folded them and put them on the ground. With barely a pause, he shifted. He scampered up the dumpster, and a new smell hit him, one he didn't recognize. He looked into the bin with blurry eyes wondering just what was that smell.

Rafe couldn't focus as well with his rat eyes as with his human eyes, but he was very sensitive to motion. So when something began to move, he hesitated a moment, his human curiosity stronger than his rat flight mechanism.

The cat took him with one leap, teeth piercing his neck, claws grabbing purchase in his sides. Together, they went over the edge of the dumpster and onto the concrete alleyway.

Panic filled his mind. He could actually feel the cat's teeth grating against his neck bones. Struggling to get away, his feet got some purchase, and he pulled himself along with the cat still on top, now with its hind legs scoring Rafe's flanks.

Shift, shift! His mind screamed at him. He tried to calm himself, tried to slow his breathing, but with a yowling cat some 20 times his size trying to kill him, his heart rate was pounding. When he felt a tingling shoot through his body, stronger than the pain of teeth and claws, he knew one of the cat's teeth had found its way through a neck joint and into his spinal chord.

With a superhuman (superrat?) effort, he tore free of the cat and managed to jump forward until he was at the base of the wall separating the mall from the storage units in back. He turned to look at his tormentor.

Unfocussed vision or not, the cat looked enormous as it stalked back up to him. Rafe knew he should shift, but he was paralyzed. When the inevitable pounce came, he tried to wheel and run, but the cat was too fast. It had him again. The claws dug into him, but the jaws missed the neck and closed over his shoulders this time.

Rafe wasn't sure he could break free again. It never dawned on him to fight back, to bite at the cat. He just wanted to get away. Now though, shifting seemed like his only option. But how could he shift when he couldn't even concentrate, he couldn't even think?

Ms. Baumgardner's lessons on breath control came back to him. Since he could already shift, he had given them only lip service, playing along with the charade. But some of them had sunken in. He let himself go, trying to forget the cat, trying to forget that he was close to his end. He quit struggling.

The cat felt him quit, and it stopped its attack. It stood up, Rafe dangling from its jaws. Rafe was only dimly aware of being carried down the alleyway, and that respite allowed him to gain control of his breathing. He calmed himself. And shifted.

The cat yowled again, this time in fear, as its jaws were suddenly wrenched open when a 6'2" human appeared between them. It retreated a few steps, its back arched and fur standing on end. In a split second, it turned and ran down the alley and disappeared around the corner.

Rafe lay on the ground, for a moment, gathering himself. He reached up to his neck and felt the puncture marks there and the blood coming from them, a blood flow which was already stopping. He had long claw marks on his sides as well, but the blood had already stopped flowing from them as well.

Up to now, shifting had been fun, an adventure. He had never really considered anything untowards happening. Now it sunk in that being a were was not a carte blanche in this world. He still had to consider actions and consequences.

He got up, went to his clothes, and got dressed. Still shaking from nervous relief, he started back home, peering around the corner first to see if the cat was still there. He wasn't sure when he would feel like shifting again.

Passing the McDonalds, he could see Jenny at the counter, waiting for a customer, or maybe waiting for him. He walked on.

Chapter 12
back in class

Rafe had circled this day in the syllabus very early on. Today's subject was animal forms.

Mr. Peterson had gone back to review some of the early history, things he had already taught, but now he was encroaching on some new territory.

"So from the wall paintings, from broken pieces of clay images, it is evident that our early ancestors took many more forms than we take today. Who can give me a possible reason for that?"

As normal, the class was silent. Mr. Peterson rolled his eyes and muttered, "Why do I even bother to ask?"

"OK, Charles Darwin anyone? Survival of the Fittest?"

"'Cause other animals are weaker?" Rob G. ventured.

Mr. Peterson looked surprised. "Well, yes, Mr. Goodpastor, in so many words. Well done."

Rob looked around the class with a smile on his face. It was a rather surprised smile that he had gotten something right, but a smile none-the-less.

"What we believe is that only certain forms have a proven ability to survive on their own. Wolves, of course. Bears. Lions. Tigers. People who shifted to rabbits, for example, became prey not only of other weres, but also to every hunter in the forest. Wererabbits might be stronger and more robust than a normal rabbit, but still, a larger were, or even a larger normal wolf or other predator could kill one. So these weres were hunted and killed before they could pass on their genes. Eventually, these lines died out."

Rafe thought about the cat which had attacked him. He had managed to escape that, but hearing this, he knew he had been lucky.

"What about Turner? He's a rat?" Of course, it was Trevor who asked that.

Rafe just ignored him, but he was interested in the answer.

Jonathan P. Brazee

"Well, it is hard to completely kill off a line, and when people intermarry, well some recessive genes survived, only to pop up at various times. But generally, it was the larger carnivores and predators who survived. Very few herbivore lines survived, and most of them are of the larger type, such as elephants and rhinos. You have all heard of Mr. Marten, in the Manitoba Tribe, of course?" They students all nodded. "Well, Mr. Marten is the only known beaver form in the world. Beavers used to be more common amongst the Native Americans, but the form has seemed to die out over the last hundred years or so. Whether this had something to do with the form itself or the dwindling population of Native Americans, well, we just don't know."

"But it is not just the carnivore-herbivore divide. Size also comes into play. We tend to shift into forms about our own human size. Yes, most bears are larger than their human size, and wolves can be a bit over or under, but like-sized human-animal pairing is the most common. It is much harder and takes much more energy to change into something much larger, or much smaller, for that matter, than your human form. Changing into an elephant, say, takes a huge amount of energy, and a wereelephant can even starve to death if he or she changes too frequently."

Did that explain his intense hunger each time he changed, wondered Rafe? It sort of made sense. His rat form was much, much smaller than his human form. He bet the difference in mass was more than if a person shifted into an elephant.

"But no one has been able to tell me how a person shifts into an elephant, or a bear, for that matter. What about Conservation of Mass?" asked Kat. "Science is science."

"That is a question that has stymied us for years," their teacher replied. "The short answer is, no one knows. The longer answer is that we have been trying to find that very thing out. All we know is that relatively few people change into forms which are far different in size, and those who do, much more energy is expended. Also, arthritis, which is the one disease which seems to really affect us, takes a much greater toll on our larger shifters, and the more often they shift, the worse the arthritis as they grow older."

"And then there is brain size. A smaller brain in the animal form seems to affect cognitive thinking. Some people think that our raptor brethren might be even a different, unique branch of the family tree. They don't seem to be bothered by the change in size, and they don't suffer from arthritis. But they do have a different experience after shifting. Ms. Moore, you have shifted already at Ft. Collins. Can you tell us how you feel when you shift? Is your personality the same?"

She shifted in her seat. "No, sir. When I shift, I sort of zone out some. I'm still there, but more as an observer. I feel like an eagle who is partly a person, not like what you tell me, a person who is wearing a wolf body."

"Precisely. Because of the smaller brain size, and perhaps they might have evolved differently as well, wereeagles and hawks are more eagle and hawk, if I can put it that way, than the rest of us are wolf, bear, or coyote. The brain may just not be big enough to house the entire person in there. We don't know."

"But what about Turner? His rat brain must be about the size of a pea!"

The rest of the class laughed, but Mr. Peterson looked thoughtful. "Good question. Mr. Turner, you made your second shift last week, right?"

No wanting to look too slow, Rafe had shifted in his last class with Ms. Baumgarder. "Yes sir."

"Did you feel any different, like you were not yourself."

"No sir. I felt normal. Like me."

"Hmm. Interesting. We might want to look into that once you are completely comfortable with shifting." He looked back up. "OK, back on track. Finally, we have location. The only sea forms we know are the selkies. Even today, the selkies keep to themselves despite being members of the United Tribes. But why only seals? Why not dolphins, or whales for that matter?"

"How can a whale shift? He would be stuck wherever he was when he shifted."

"Mr. Goodpastor, I am astounded. That is twice in one day. Whatever has gotten into you, keep it up! You are right. Only the seals can survive on land. If there ever were any weredolphins or whales, well, they would have probably died before they could get into the water. Maybe a few managed to be near water, or they could survive until they reverted back to human form. But the facts are that the selkies are the only known sea forms amongst the United Tribes."

Rafe sat there quietly and thought about what he had been told. He didn't buy the brain size argument. He felt the same when he was a rat. But the big question was just why he was a rat. What Mr. Peterson said made sense, but how had the stars aligned just right (or just wrong) to make him the only known wererat?

Chapter 13
Rafe's birthday

"Open it, open it," Tabitha squealed, excitement rising.

"I don't know, maybe I should keep it for my next birthday," he teased back.

"Noooo! You have to open it now! That's the rules!"

"OK, OK." He tore the paper off to reveal a plain brown box inside. "Oh, thanks Tabby Cat. My own box! Just what I wanted!"

She punched him in the arm. "No! Inside the box. You have to open it!"

Rafe looked around the room. His Gammy refused to participate, but his parents, his older sister, Jaira, and his aunt had joined Tabitha to help him celebrate his 17th birthday. After a delicious meal of pot roast (with the Lipton Onions Soup mix on top), he was opening up his presents. He looked at Tabitha, hands clasped together in front of her chin, eyes riveted on the box in his hand.

He ruffled her hair, which did nothing to break her concentration. Opening the outer box, his stomach fell. There, in a blue box with "Ratatouille" blazoned on the cardboard, and staring out through a clear plastic front, was a stuffed rat.

"It's Remy!" she told him with delight. "I picked him myself!"

He looked up at the others. His mother had a slightly uncomfortable look on her face, but she rolled her shoulders and raised her eyebrows in an apology, motioning with her finger to Tabitha. No one else would catch his eyes.

Tabitha couldn't contain herself. She reached over, opened the package, and took out the chef hat-wearing blue rat. "See? Just like in the movie. And he's got a cooking spoon!" She tried to fit the spoon into its hand.

She suddenly looked up at Rafe. "You like him, right?"

He had to smile. "Of course, Tabby Cat, because you gave him to me."

She gave him a fierce hug around his neck. "He's my favorite cook, and you're my favorite brother, so I wanted you to have him. Maybe next time you change, you can cook for me like him."

Rafe was surprised to feel a lump in his throat. "Sure thing." He leaned forward to whisper into her ear, "But don't let Jaira know he's your favorite cook. She might feel bad."

Tabitha's eyes grew round and her mouth dropped open. She wheeled around and rushed to Jaira, hugging her leg. "Jaira, I meant for a boy cook, not you!"

The gathering broke out into laughter as Jaira reassured Tabitha. Rafe opened the rest of his presents, then cut the Black Forest cake Jaira had baked, distributing the pieces around. He was eating it when Tabitha came back over and offered hopefully, "I think maybe Remy can get lost with all these people. If you want, I can watch him for now, then I can give him back to you when you go upstairs."

"OK, you watch him for me." He watched her happily pick up the rat and sit on the floor, already lost in her play.

His dad came to sit down beside him. "You know, she didn't mean anything by that. By picking a toy rat for a present."

"I know. And nothing's wrong about it anyway. It is what it is. Nothing to be ashamed of, right?"

"That's the attitude! If you say it, you'll believe it." He clapped him on the shoulder.

Rafe looked up to catch Claire's eyes. She was listening, and when their eyes met, she rolled hers, then smiled. His father's words, while he meant them to be supportive, reflected his true feelings, that he felt Rafe's animal form was inferior. And Claire understood that as well.

Rafe had come to terms with his inner rat. That was who he was. Did he wish he was a tiger like his mom? Or a wolf like his father and sister? Sure he did. But he wasn't. And nothing was going to change that. It was best just to accept what he was and to make the best of it.

Chapter 14
still more classes

As they straggled into class, each student's attention was drawn to a series of old prints up on the walls. There were wolves eating people, manlike wolves tearing off limbs, people holding down a wolf with ropes with an axeman ready to cut off its head, wolves consigned to the fires. Most were simplistic prints of wood carvings, but a few were prints of newer, but still old oil paintings, the detail exquisitely rendered. In one, a large wolf, the fear evident in its eyes, cowered before a knight whose lance was poised to skewer it.

Mr. Peterson shambled in, then took his place in front of the class.

"Have no doubt about it. We have enemies in this world, enemies who want to exterminate us. As you can see from the art around us," he gestured with one arm, encompassing the prints, "other men fear and loath us. And, to be fair, not always without reason. As I told you before, the United Tribes was formed to control our more wild members, to keep us out of the public notice, to keep us as mere figments of Hollywood's imagination."

"Most people don't believe in us. Oh, many want to believe, but in their hearts, they believe we are fictional beings. Of course, some of the claims about us are farfetched, like we are invincible. We may be tough, and we may be unusually healthy, but we can be killed."

"Who here has heard of God's Judgment?" he asked.

"Isn't that that weird church that pickets dead soldier's funerals for being gay or something?" offered Kat.

"Yes, that's one of their attention-getting stunts. To be more specific, they picket the soldier's funerals claiming that God is killing our soldiers as punishment for the country accepting gays into society. Regardless of what they profess, though, the group is perhaps our most implacable enemy here in this country."

"But why? We aren't gay!" asked Trevor, before hurriedly looking at Rob S. "I mean, we're not a gay group. I mean, not all of us."

"Gay or straight is not on their agenda. They come from a long line of werewolf hunters. This is just their latest guise."

"So why the gay thing?"

"Well, do you really think they could raise much money telling people they were fighting werewolves?"

Trevor thought about it for a second, then nodded his understanding.

"They protest against gays, against Jews, against Arabs to pick up donations from the other crazies. But their real focus is on us. They firmly believe that God has given them that task."

"But we are Christian, too. I mean most of us here," interjected Erica. "I am. I go to church every Sunday."

"To them, anyone who fails to toe the line with their rather stringent creed is a fallen Christian, maybe even more sinful than a Jew, Hindu, or Muslim. I think they would happily shoot through the Pope himself if that bullet would then take out one of us."

"There are other groups, of course, and certain individuals, but in the US, God's Judgment remains our deadliest enemy. We've been lucky here, and you are probably all too young to remember their last attack on one of us, but other tribes have felt their sting."

"So why don't we just take them out?" Trevor was getting somewhat worked up.

"Oh, we have taken action against them. And we will continue to do so. But there always seems to be more of them. And their headquarters is rather impenetrable to us, given that it is made with silver intertwining every structure there. In this, all the legends about weres are true. We can't tolerate silver."

Rafe perked up at that. He had never really realized that, and come to think of it, his house was entirely devoid of silver. It had just never occurred to him to notice it or wonder why.

"We can't?"   asked Jorge and Lief, almost in unison. Evidently, Rafe wasn't the only one who hadn't realized that.

"Well, I guess it pertains to today's lesson. Go to page 106 in your books, please." Mr. Peterson waited while books were opened and the page found.   "This is an image of the silver molecule. As you can read along with me, it has 47 electrons and 61 neutrons. Something about this construction seems to interfere with our ability to shift."

"It doesn't make too much sense," put in Kat.

"No, it doesn't. Or I should say we just don't understand it. But silver is a germicide. It can be used to keep swimming pools clean of algae, which is a higher organism than germs. Even non-shifting humans can suffer from argyria from too much contact with silver and silver compounds. It turns their skin grey and affects the mucosal system. When you take into account that silver has the highest thermal and electrical conductivity of any metal, well, our nerves are firing millions, or rather billions of electrical impulse when we shift, so maybe it does make sense. We just don't have a grasp of it yet."

"Regardless, silver can keep us from shifting into our animal form or back into our human form. This inability to shift can last for several hours after simple contact, what we call a 'silver burn.'   And silver can constrict our healing capabilities. Last week, we spoke about our health advantages, how we can heal from broken bones, from falls, from cuts very quickly. How we don't get infections. That's why we are so hard to kill. But a silver bullet, for example, even if it doesn't kill us immediately, can retard our healing, and that can lead us to bleed out and die. Prolonged contact with silver usually renders us unconscious."

"Oh, and yes, touching silver hurts like hell!" he added with a little more emotion than he usually used in his lectures.

The class looked aghast at Mr. Peterson, shocked at his language.

"Well, it does. I know from experience," he said sheepishly.

"You said that this God's Judgment made their home out of silver?" asked Kat.

"Well, silver bars, no. I imagine that would be extremely expensive. But we think they have sprayed the outside of all their buildings with a silver colloidal solution. And from our tests with that, yes, even that is enough to stop us. It may not kill us, but the pain is intense, and it can knock us out."

"Um...Mr. Peterson...what does it take to kill us? I mean, if they come after us?" asked Trevor, obviously still worked up.

"Most of that should be obvious. Cut off our head, well, we're dead. Burn us, cut out our heart, crush us, drown us-- just about all the things that would kill a Static human. If it would kill one of them right away, it will probably kill us, too. Where we have the advantage is that not only are we seemingly immune to most diseases, but if it doesn't kill us right away, we have a very good chance to recover, and recover very quickly. Add the fact that we are stronger and faster, well, we're pretty hard to kill."

Rafe shuddered. He had no intention of getting anywhere close to God's Judgment, nor anyone else who had something against the werewolves. Or wererats. A nice quiet life was more his style.

Chapter 15
three weeks later

"Who're ya chatting with?" asked Claire in a singsong voice, throwing herself over the back of the couch to land with a thud next to Rafe.

"Uh, nobody!" he responded, trying to turn his iPhone so she couldn't see.

"I bet it's a girl!" she said again, half singing, half speaking. She snatched the phone out of his hand and jumped off the couch, glee as she peeked at the screen. "Jenny? Whose that? We don't have a Jenny here. We've got a Jen, one n, but no Jenny." She looked confused.

"You don't know her." He tried to take the phone back.

"Honey, I know EVERYONE here. Which tribe is she from? And when did you meet her? You haven't gone presenting yet."

Rafe grimaced. Now that he had finished Revelations, he was expected to go "presenting," that is, travel to the other tribes and be introduced to any eligible young ladies there. He wasn't looking forward to that. Most people here had come to accept his animal form, even if no one outside of his Revelations class had seen it since First Shift. He didn't really feel like dealing with whole new tribes with that fact.

Suddenly Claire's eyes widened and her mouth dropped open. "Ohh, she's a jello? Right? Right?"

Rafe jumped up and grabbed the phone. "Shh! Be quiet!"

"Oh, brother, you're already going out with a jello!" She doubled up, hand in front of her mouth, trying not to laugh. "Dad's going to throw a fit!"

"Nothing wrong with it. Uncle Taylor married a Static," he put emphasis on the label.

"Yeah, but that's because he searched all the tribes first. He didn't marry her until he was thirty or even older. You haven't even tried yet." She paused a moment. "You mean, you're going to marry her?"

"No, no! She's just a friend. That's all."

She sat back down close to him, as if a fellow conspirator in some dastardly plot. "You got a picture?"

"Uh, no, not yet."

"What kind of boyfriend doesn't keep a picture of his girlfriend?"

"She's not my girlfriend! I told you, we're just friends!" he protested.

"Well, is she cute? What's she look like?"

"She's, well, she's..." he let that trail off. He liked Jenny, but she was not the trophy girlfriend. He knew it shouldn't matter, but given his fall in status, he wasn't sure he wanted to parade her around, even if she wouldn't have been a Static.

His sister didn't seem to notice his hesitation. "Where'd you meet her? I mean, you don't have much contact with jellos, right?"

"She works at McDonalds," he admitted quietly.

"The one on McCormick?"

"Yeah, that one."

She grabbed his arm and started to pull him up. "You know, that text said she's at work. Come on baby bro, we're going over there so I can see her."

He tried to pull back down. "No, she's at work now. I can't bother her."

"I'm not going to take her out of work! We can just order something to eat, and I can see her. Maybe say hi." When he didn't move, she added, "You don't have a choice here, you know. You're coming, or I'm going over there and ask everyone to point her out to me."

That had even more potential for embarrassment, so he reluctantly agreed. "OK, but don't make a scene. You've got to promise me that."

"OK, OK! Put on your shoes, and let's get out of here!" She grabbed her purse and waited impatiently while he laced up his New Balances. "I swear, you are the slowest guy I know!"

"Mom! I'm taking Rafe out for awhile," she shouted out, obviously not expecting a reply. She flung open the door and walked around their mother's Suburban to her car, holding the key out at arm's length towards it as if pushing the unlock would somehow work better if it was two feet closer.

Rafe slid into the passenger's seat of his sister's new Mazda 2. It was a tight fit for his bulk, but he had to admit, it was a sweet ride. The bright green might be distracting, but when Claire had let him drive it around the neighborhood a few days before, he rather liked its zip.

She left the headlights on bright, despite the many street lights illuminating the way. When they left the development and hit the feeder road, an oncoming driver flashed his lights at her, which she ignored as she continued her interrogation of Rafe.

Rafe tried to stay non-committal to her prying, thinking that she was being more junior high than a university student. But her joy at good gossip was a little infectious. He realized he missed her in the house during the week. It was better when she came home for the weekend.

As they passed Foo-foo dog's house, he looked out the window, wondering if the dog would make an appearance. Oddly enough, he felt a little disappointed when the dog didn't show.

They pulled out on the main road and then into the back of the McDonald's parking lot. Claire liked to park away from the other cars, not wanting to get her doors dinged by others. Rafe felt a bit apprehensive as he stepped out of the car. He realized he probably should have texted Jenny before coming over, but it was too late.

He and Claire went in the side door by the drive-through. The familiar deep-fryer smell pervaded his senses, something even his human nose could detect. Jenny was serving a woman with a small child and didn't see him at first. When she caught his eye, she smiled, then frowned a bit when Claire grabbed his arm and pulled him to the register.

"Hi Jenny! I'm Claire!" She held out her hand, and Jenny automatically took it. "So you like my little brother, huh?"

Jenny's smile came back, but she protested, "Oh, we're just friends. He comes in here, you know, a lot." She tried to push her hair into a degree of compliance.

"Oh, don't worry about me. I think it's cute."

Jenny looked a little confused at that, and Rafe rolled his eyes. Claire needed to work on her social skills, he thought. He interrupted and asked Claire what she wanted to eat.

"Oh, just a diet is fine," she told him.

"OK, Jenny, a diet and a large fries," he relayed.

"Only a large fries for you? You always have two meals when you come."

Rafe realized that this was the first time since his First Shift that he had come in without shifting or getting ready to shift. He had already eaten dinner at home, and he just wasn't that hungry.

"Ah, gotta watch my weight, you know," he said, patting his flat stomach.

"Yeah, right," she replied, but she rang them both up. "That'll be $1.91, please."

"What, no discount for your boyfriend?"

Both Rafe and Jenny looked up in embarrassment.

"I'm just kidding! Jeeze! You guys can't take a joke!" she said teasingly.

Jenny shrugged and went to get them their food.

"I though you weren't going to embarrass me," Rafe whispered to her.

"Ah, I couldn't resist. I have to have a little fun, you know." She reached up to ruffle his hair.

Jenny brought them their mini-meal. "It was nice meeting you, Claire."

"Yeah, nice meeting you, too," Claire replied.

They took the tray and found an empty table as the man who had been standing in back of them took his place to order.

"Well, she has a nice smile," Claire told him as they sat down.

Rafe looked at her closely, but she seemed genuine as she tore off the top of the paper wrapper on her straw, then blew the wrapper at him. It curved at the last second to miss him. He knew that Jenny was not a runway model, and he was wondered if that was the only complimentary thing that Claire could think of to say. He knew he shouldn't be so sensitive. He liked Jenny, and that is what mattered.

Claire ate half of his fries, but he hadn't been that hungry in the first place. They got up, took their tray to the bin, and walked by the counter.

"Take care, Jenny. Maybe we can meet sometime when you're not working. And without my little bro here. You know, girls night out."

"Uh, sure, I guess." Jenny seemed unsure of herself.

Rafe merely raised his eyebrows and mouthed out "Sorry!"

Claire took his arm as they entered the parking lot. "You know, she seems sweet, but she's a jello. And before you get serious, you need to meet more girls from the tribes."

Rafe didn't bother to answer. He was not in a serious relationship, and he wasn't ready for one. He just liked having someone who would not look down on him for being a rat.

Claire reached out again with her key and beeped the car unlocked.

"Excuse me. Can you help me?"

Rafe and Claire turned around to see a casually dressed middle-aged man in back of them. Slightly balding, he seemed pleasant enough, but was clearly befuddled.

"Yes?" asked Rafe.

"I got off the interstate to get some gas and find someplace to eat. Now I can't seem to find my way back. I think I've seen this McDonalds three times now, and I've got a long way to go to get home. It's my daughter's birthday, you know, and I really need to make it back. Can you point me in the right direction?"

"The interstate? You're really out of the way, you know. It's got to be, what, 7 or 8 miles away," Claire told him.

"Seven or 8 miles? Wow! I've got to be a real idiot! My wife always tells me to ask directions, but well, you know...," he replied in an embarrassed tone. He pulled out a folded map from his back pocket and unfolded it. "Maybe you can show me on here?"

He made an effort to read it. "It's hard to read it now, but maybe we can see it better under the light by your car? That's it over there, right? I saw the lights flash when you unlocked it." He walked over to the Mazda and laid out the map.

Rafe hurried over, anxious to help. He felt Claire behind him. Another car pulled alongside of them and stopped despite there being many empty parking spots at this end of the lot. The rear door closest to them opened and a young man in blue jeans and a white t-shirt got out. Rafe gave him a cursory glance before looking back at the map.

"OK, get into the car." The lost man's voice shifted down and became much more serious.

Rafe looked up at him to see the man pointing a large handgun at them. He used the barrel of the gun to indicate the car which had pulled up alongside of them.

"These are the proverbial silver bullets, so please don't make me use them." He still looked like the harmless family man who had stopped them for directions, but his voice belonged to someone more fervent and harder. "And now. No one has seen us yet, but if anyone does, I swear I will blow you both away right here and now."

Rafe froze for a moment, the instinctively, started to shift. Claire's hand grasping his arm made him stop.

"What are you doing? What do you want?" she asked the man, a note of panic in her voice.

"Now. In the car. You'll get all your questions answered soon. But IN...THE...CAR...NOW!"

He waved the gun in their faces. The muzzle of the gun looked awfully big to Rafe. He looked away for a moment and only then noticed that the young man also had a gun. He looked far more nervous than the older man, and that scared Rafe more. *What do they want with us?*

Rafe was scared, to be sure. But not as much as the situation might warrant, and that surprised him. The young man reached out and grabbed Claire's arm, pulling her towards the car.

"You have about 5 seconds to get in the car, or I start shooting. Don't be waiting for the Lone Ranger, 'cause he ain't a'coming. One...two...,"

"Come on Steve. We don't have a choice," Claire told him. She took a step to the waiting blue sedan and climbed into the back.

"Smart girl. And you?"

Rafe merely nodded and climbed into the back. There was another man in the back against the far window. He was a large man, overweight, with a full beard. If was hard to see more with the only light coming from the lights in the parking lot. The younger man got in after Rafe, pushing him up against Claire. He could feel her trembling.

The first man got into the front seat. As he closed the door, the driver started backing up, then pulled forward and out onto McCormick Avenue.

Turning back to look at him, he said, "I want to thank you for getting such a bright car, Miss Turner. Makes it that much easier to track you."

Rate felt Claire deflate next to him. They knew who she was. The question was who were they?

He turned to Rafe. "And unless you are Stephen Parkinson, which I rather doubt as you don't look like you are in your 50's, I don't think your name really is Steve. No, you are undoubtedly Rhett Sykes." Even in the shifting light of moving streetlights, Rafe could see the self-satisfied expression on the man's round face.

They thought he was Rhett? But Rhett was at least three or four years older than him, and they looked nothing alike. He started to deny it when Claire pinched his side hard.

And now, I imagine you are wondering just who we are. I am Deacon Samuel Price of the Church of God's Judgment, and you are demon spawn."

Chapter 16
15 minutes and 10 miles later

The deacon had been going on about the evil that had taken over the country, that evil being the demons who can shift shapes and perform Satan's will. Rafe was steeling himself to keep denying everything. How could they prove he was a were unless he shifted?

"Turn left here," the deacon informed the driver. They drove in relative silence down a dirt road, bouncing up and down as the worn-out shocks in the sedan could not compensate for the rough conditions.

The car pulled to a stop. The young man, who hadn't said a word during the short trip, got out, motioning for Rafe to follow him. Rafe had at least 30 pounds on the young guy, and he contemplated jumping him, but with Claire with him, he didn't want to take the chance. If she could shift, then maybe she could get into the woods and escape. Better to bide his time. Then he looked up and noticed the others. There were at least 10 men and a few women waiting for them. A few looked nervous, but most seemed determined. All of them were illuminated by a series of floodlights.

The car had parked next to a large panel van in a fairly large clearing. Just at the edge of the range of the lights, trees could be seen. Rafe didn't actually know where they were, but it couldn't be that far from the furthest reaches of the Ranch. If they could just get away, they could be on tribal land.

In front of one man and woman was an odd machine. It looked to have some lights attached haphazardly on top, and in front was a bundled mass of, well, Rafe couldn't tell what.

"Miss Turner, Mister Sykes, welcome to your judgment," the deacon intoned.

"You are crazy. You know that? We're some sort of werewolf demons? Do you know how crazy that sounds?" Claire asked him, stress evident in her voice.

"Ah, Miss Turner, I know you know who we are. And I know you know that we have been your sworn hunters, the sword of the True God, for hundreds of years. We know all about werewolves, werebears, werepanthers, and the like. This is our holy mission."

Most of the others nodded in agreement. One slim, dark-haired man looked positively eager to get on with whatever was planned.

"But what if you're wrong? What if we aren't all these crazy things?" she asked the deacon.

"Well, in that case, we'll apologize and leave you be. But," he said with a smile, "we're almost never wrong."

He motioned to the two men flanking the two of them. They each took one of them by the arm and escorted them through the calf-high dried grass and into the middle of the lighted area in the clearing. Turning them to face the deacon, each man took a few steps to the side and forward.

Rafe couldn't help but think of movies like *The Great Escape*, where the Nazis gunned down the Allied prisoners. Now he was beginning to feel more frightened. He snuck a quick look over his shoulder. Maybe they could make a break that way.

"And now, my dear demons, we will see just what kind of weredemon you are."

The deacon motioned to the woman near the strange machine. She bent down and flipped a switch...

...and an unbelievably bright light lit up their very souls. This was stronger than any moonlight, any medallion. Without meaning to, in fact without being able to resist, Rafe and Claire shifted.

Rafe fell into the grass between his sister's wolf legs.

"Where is Sykes?" he could hear the deacon shout. "Fire the net!"

There was a small explosion, and Rafe could see movement in the air. He tried to jump, but suddenly he was pinned by something that burned fiercely across his back. Trapped against his sister's flank, he wiggled furiously until he fell back to the ground. Looking up, he saw his sister being held by a silver net, one with openings large enough to let a rat through, but more than fine enough to hold a wolf. With the silver around her, she could not shift back into human form. He was burned, but he thought he could shift. But what could he do against a dozen armed men? He caught his sister's eye, and she motioned with her nose towards the trees and whined. Did she want him to run?

He could hear running feet, so with one more glance at Claire, he scurried into the grass, completely hidden from the men. He ran as fast as he could until he reached the trees and scampered up the first one.

"Where is he? Damn it! Find the demon spawn! We can't let him get away!" The deacon's voice cut through the light and into the darkness.

"Here's his clothes. He changed all right," one of the others told the rest.

"Well, how can he of gotten away?" the woman on the machine yelled out.

"Maybe the moon projector was too strong. It kind of blinded me, at least," the man who had found Rafe's clothes offered. "So he could've stepped back when we were blinded, and then the net missed him." He looked apprehensively into the dark forest, then back at the deacon. "Uh, should we go after him?"

The deacon thought for a moment. "No, even with our guns, he's got the advantage there. Wolf or bear or whatever, we don't need to chance that yet. And we've got to get out of here. But maybe this is a good thing. We've left this pack alone for awhile. Now they know we're on their trail. And now we know that our moon projector works."

"What about his one?" he asked, motioning to Claire, who panted and whined under the unremitting pressure and pain of the silver net.

Deacon Samuel Price merely smiled and said, "Anton, send her back to Hell."

Rafe's vision while in his rat form was not the best, and things tended to be out of focus. But he saw clearly the slim, dark-haired man smile as he picked up what looked to be an old fashion pike, like the ones used in the middle ages. The pike's head shined with a silvery gleaming in the glare of the lights.

He sauntered up to Claire, raised the pike, and brought it down through the net and into her neck. Claire howled in agony. Again and again he struck as Rafe silently screamed. Claire's howling suddenly cut off, yet the man didn't stop. As Claire's head finally parted her body and slid down inside the net, Rafe turned, jumped off the tree branch, and ran into the darkness, not caring nor understanding just to where he was fleeing.

Chapter 17
an hour later

"You fucking useless piece of shit! You just left her like that?" Rhett charged across the clearing, shifting into his wolf.

Rafe just stood there, waiting for Rhett's jaws to close around his throat. If several others hadn't interceded, his life might have ended right there. He couldn't take his eyes off Claire's body. Once the silver net had been pulled off of her, she had reverted to her prime form in death. Her clothes had managed to stay basically intact through two shifts, and her body looked disheveled, but not too out of the ordinary. But her head had been picked up and placed a few feet away and facing her body, as if to show her lifeless eyes what had happened to her.

His father was on his knees beside her. His mother stood behind him, hands on his shoulder as he quietly sobbed.

Rafe had run mindlessly through the undergrowth after seeing Claire decapitated. It wasn't for several minutes that he was able to get ahold of his thoughts and slow down. He knew he had to get back to the tribe. And staying rat wasn't going to get him there quickly.

He shifted back into his human form and ran naked and shoeless back through the woods. He had never been in this stretch of forest before, but he knew the general direction of the tribe's lands. He wasn't conscious of his feet getting torn up, nor the cuts and scratches that grasping branches and vines inflicted on him. His body struggled to heal the cuts, but more and more were made as he plunged through anything and everything in his way. By the time he stumbled into the playground at the edge of the housing development, he was dirty and bloodied.

His goal was his home, but he was almost immediately stopped by a group of men playing basketball. He stammered out his story, and within minutes, the alarm had been raised as guys used their cells to call in help, sort of a posse. Someone threw him a pair of sweats to put on and gave him a bottle of Gatorade, which he gratefully downed. He could feel the familiar ache of a post-shift hunger, but only peripherally. He felt disembodied, as if he wasn't really there.

His father and mother were among the first few to arrive, fear on their faces. His mother hugged him tightly, then pushed him at arm's length to look at him, an unspoken question in her eyes. Rafe broke down then and cried. His mother pulled him back to her breast, tears welling up in her eyes as well.

A few voices shouted out for calm as the growing crowd began to angrily argue. They insisted that they should all go there together by car, a large unassailable group. But half-a-dozen werewolves took off their clothes and shifted, sure that their noses and fleet legs would get them to the scene quicker than the crowd could get there by car. Like wraiths, they jumped the wall surrounding the development and disappeared into the night.

Within minutes, though, five or six vehicles were there, and with the still shoeless Rafe shoved into the lead Escalade, the convoy peeled out of the development and out through the main gate. Ron Amos, who owned the Escalade, had put a revolving blue light on the roof, and leading the way, traffic laws were ignored as they sped to McCormick Avenue and then down the highway. Rafe was in the front seat, afraid he would miss the turnoff. He had them slow down for one side road, but then told Mr. Amos to keep going as he realized it wasn't the right one. He was sure they had passed it until he recognized the turn, and all the vehicles made their way down the dirt road.

Before they reached the clearing, the howls of wolves filled the air. The others had made it there first.

When they pulled into the clearing, Anna Ceres stood naked in the clearing, revealed by the oncoming car lights, looking down at the grass. The others were still in their wolf form, taking turns lifting their heads and howling. The cars pulled around each other, aiming their headlights at Anna. Slowly, the all got out of the cars and walked up, Rafe's mother and father being escorted by some of the others. Those who had shifted into their animals started to shift back.

Rafe was in shock as the others starting yelling and vowing revenge. Why did he run? Why couldn't he have done anything? If he had been anything other than a rat, could he have attacked? There were a bunch of them, true, but as a tiger, a bear, or even an elephant? Could he have saved Claire? But instead of anything useful, he was only a rat. A rat who ran.

So when Rhett started to attack him, he not only accepted it, he welcomed it. He needed to be punished. As much as he was capable of feeling, he was almost disappointed when the others pulled Rhett back.

Rafe's uncle and Andy Filipović hustled him back to his parent's Suburban and shoved him in the back seat as most of the others merely glared at him. Even in his human form, Rafe could almost smell their contempt. Looking through the windshield, he could see several people gently lifting up Claire's body and taking her to Mr. Amos' Escalade. He couldn't see who had her head, but he didn't really want to see that.

He sat in a daze while people loaded back into the cars. He was in a daze as they made their way slowly back to the development. He was in a daze while the posse met up with the rest of the tribe in the community center. Nothing seemed to register.

Led by Rhett, one faction of the tribe wanted to launch some sort of attack on the God's Judgment. Others argued for a more reasoned and thought-out approach. Rafe heard the comments made by some others blaming him, but it was almost as if they were talking about someone else. He felt that he was neither human nor rat. He was nobody.

His mother finally looked up and seemed to notice what was going on with her son. She leaned toward Jaira and whispered in her ear. Jaira nodded and got up, coming to Rafe. Taking him by the hand, she led him out of the recreation room and back towards their home, away from the accusing eyes of the others.

Chapter 18
several hours later

Rafe lay in bed awake. How could he sleep? He had been going over every detail of what had happened. What could he have done differently?

If he hadn't been texting Jenny, none of this would have happened. Claire would still be alive. If he had only been more aware at the McDonalds, if he had ignored that man when he asked for help, she would still be alive. And most of all, if he were a real were, someone with some use, he could have fought them off and saved Claire. His useless animal form betrayed him, betrayed Claire.

Rafe realized that Claire could have shifted and bolted away, taking her chances with a silver bullet hitting somewhere vital even if she was hit at all. But she knew Rafe was a rat, and as a rat, he couldn't get away like she could. She had stayed to protect him, her little brother. Rafe knew that because of that choice, she was dead, murdered. It really was his fault.

A couple of hours after being led out of the community center, he heard the door open downstairs and muted voices. After a bit, someone, his mother or father, opened his bedroom door, but he never acknowledged that. He just lay there in his misery.

The longer he lay there, the more he seemed to return to himself. His thoughts became more normal, and focused, more belonging to him. But they did nothing to alleviate his sense of guilt. If anything, his more rational thoughts cemented his opinion that he was useless, a tribe member only by technicality.

His rat seemed to realize this, too. He felt zero presence within him, zero yearning to shift. The rat inside seemed dead.

Rafe knew that his standing within the tribe had been largely based on his family. Most people carefully ignored reference to his rat. Others made jokes and comments behind his back or even to his face. Now, with what had just happened, he knew his standing would be even lower. He was a nobody. He felt another, separate pang of guilt for even considering this. His sister had been murdered, and he worried about his standing within the tribe?

Sometime just before dawn, something clicked in his mind. He couldn't imagine facing the others, facing his family, facing Rhett. So he wouldn't face them. He was useless as a were. So he would leave them. Making that decision lifted a load off his mind.

Getting up, he got dressed and grabbed his backpack. He stuffed in some extra clothes and another pair of shoes. Looking around his room, there was not much else he wanted. He was about to leave when he saw Remy standing on his nightstand.

He felt his first pang of misgiving. What about Tabitha? She had lost her big sister tonight, although she slept blissfully unaware of that yet. Was it fair to her to take her big brother away, too?

He picked up the stuffed toy. Remy was a rat, but one who could achieve his dreams. But, and this was a huge but, this was real life, not Hollywood, not Pixar. Some things just had to be accepted as out-of-reach.

Steeling his resolve, he quietly stepped out of his room and down the hall. He could hear murmurings from inside his parent's bedroom. Evidently, sleep was slow in coming to more than just him. As quite as he could, he opened the door to Tabitha's room.

She lay in peaceful repose, lost in her little girl dreams. She would learn that those dreams were a far nicer place than reality, a reality where her sister could have her head cut off simply because she was different.

Rafe carefully placed Remy on her nightstand, then leaned over and gave her a butterfly kiss on her cheek.

"Take care, Tabby Cat," he whispered.

He turned and left before he could change his mind, going down the stairs, thankful that Gammy was not up yet. He opened the front door and stepped out, ready to leave his life behind. As he marched on, he didn't notice the upstairs window where a little girl, clutching a stuffed blue rat, watched him leave.

Part 2

Chapter 19
12 years later

"Hey, babe, I'm home!"   Rafe closed the door to their apartment, threw his books on the small, beat-up credenza, and flopped down on the overstuffed pink chair. MJ didn't acknowledge his entrance, but then again, she rarely did.

He looked at her as she typed away on her laptop, totally engrossed in her words. As usual, she was wearing her old, worn grey cotton men's shorts and a threadbare pink t-shirt. Neither did much to hide her rather impressive figure. He sat for a moment and wondered for the umpteenth time how he had managed to attract her.

Oh, Rafe knew she had faults. Her social skills were lacking, to put it mildly. She could be extremely self-centered. But from a physical standpoint, MJ was the proverbial knockout. Her sister was some sort of tv star back in Taiwan, but when comparing photos, Rafe thought MJ was much prettier. At about 5' 9", she was quite slender, but had fairly prominent breasts, and Rafe never got tired of looking at her.

Rafe had gotten used to nudity while with the tribe. Back in his classes with Mrs. Baumgardner, he and his fellow students had been nude as they practiced their mind-calming exercises, but MJ's complete lack of body self-consciousness both attracted and still excited him, even after living together with her for almost 5 months.

He had met MJ in class. They had been assigned as lab partners, and with her ever practical mind, she had insisted that they spend as much time as possible in order to maximize their grades. The first time she came to his apartment to study, she just never seemed to leave. Rafe couldn't actually pinpoint when they started "living together." It just sort of happened, like the first time they made love. To be honest, Rafe didn't know exactly what MJ felt for him, and he didn't know if he loved her, but for now, the arrangement seemed to work out.

He really didn't know that much about her. He knew she had married an American in Taiwan, moved to the US, then left him after several years. She got her undergraduate degree from San Jose State in biology, then started her masters here at UC San Diego where they met. With his own convoluted path to get there and her married life, both were several years older than the rest of their classmates.

Rafe knew the other students thought her rather strange, but maybe that is why they got along together. One oddball for another.

He leaned back and watched her type. She had no room for romance, couldn't understand a joke if it hit her between the eyes, and was somewhat oblivious as to the motivations of others, but she suited him fine. She was only his second girlfriend (he felt awkward using that term, though, which she never used and seemed sort of junior high school-ish.)

His met his first girlfriend at his GED classes. Sveta was a social bee, completely opposite from MJ. With her long red hair and complete love of fashion, Rafe had been smitten. He gave his virginity to Sveta, and he was sure they would live together forever. But Alexander had done them in.

Alexander was Sveta's pomeranian, and that dog truly hated him. The first few times Rafe had gone over to her apartment, the dog had gone crazy, much to Sveta's concern. When Rafe tried to stay over one night, the dog, which normally slept with his mistress, would not cease his barking and scratching at the bedroom door. Sveta worried aloud about what was wrong with the little guy, but how could Rafe just casually mention that dogs could smell out weres, and that he was a wererat (even a "reformed" wererat?) Sveta at first insisted that they try to get the two of them to like each other, but a girl's dog was evidently more important than her boyfriend, and they quickly drifted apart.

Thinking about Sveta brought out a contemplative mood. As he idly watched MJ type, he thought back on the path he had taken since leaving the tribe. It hadn't been easy. Hitchhiking around the country until he ran out of money in Portland. That was his low spot, but he was surprised to find so many runaways there, kids who showed him the ropes. He balked when a few of the other boys told him he needed to sell himself to make money, but he had almost given in to the inevitability when a pastor at one of the local churches reached out to him.

He never really wanted to be on the street, so he eagerly grasped at this lifeline. Pastor Mark got him a bed at the Porch Light Youth Shelter, and with their help, he landed a job as a stockboy at Trader Joe's. It may not have been his dream situation, but it was better than the alternative.

After a promotion at work and his own small (very small) apartment, he felt like he had a place in society. That was the first time he called home. His parents begged him to come back, but he wasn't ready for that, so he merely assured them that he was fine. After that, he tried to call them once a month to say hi. He particularly enjoyed his chats with Tabitha.

He slowly realized that he actually liked working at Trader Joe's, but without a high school diploma, he knew he couldn't advance. So he got back in touch with Pastor Mark who enrolled him in a GED program, almost four years since he had left the tribal school.

Breezing through that, he figured why not continue, so he started taking classes at the Portland Community College. Despite still being a loner, he found out he liked college more than stocking olive oil and inexpensive wines. The mental challenge gave him back a degree of purpose. And he did well, well enough to get a need-based scholarship to Oregon State. That led to a degree in Marine Biology, and that led to his getting accepted into graduate school at Scripps Institute of Technology on the UC San Diego campus.

And so here he was, a year from getting his degree, sitting on his beat up chair, watching his brilliant and beautiful girlfriend type away. Not too bad for a boy who came within a gnat's hair of selling his body in order to survive.

He got up, walking to MJ, and gave her a small peck on the top of her head. She raised one hand in a half-wave, eyes never leaving her screen. Rafe smiled and walked back into the bedroom, taking off his jeans to slide on a pair of shorts. He had quite a bit of work to do, and sitting there reflecting on his past was not going to get it done.

He took the other side of the kitchen table and plugged in his Macbook Pro. Still more used to his older HP, he knew he had only gotten the Mac because most of the other students had them, and he felt he needed one to be considered a serious student, perhaps one who should be considered for the Ph.D. program.

As usual, he first checked his hotmail. For the last several years, he and Tabitha had kept in touch regularly through e-mail and chats. Until nine months ago, after she had had her First Shift, those and calls had been their only way to communicate. But when she completed Revelations, she had come to San Diego to visit for a week. Rafe had been amazed to see the young woman his little Tabby Cat had become. It had been a good week of catching up.

And yes, there was an e-mail from her. He clicked it open.

Rafe,

Your phone is off again. Call me as soon as you get this.

Tabitha

He grimaced as he pulled out his phone. Despite his use of high-tech instruments in his academic life, he had turned his back on many of the conveniences of the modern world. He very rarely used his phone to text, and he was intelligent enough to realize that could be because he associated texting with his text messages to Jenny which precipitated both Claire's murder and then the disaster that followed, as ridiculous as that sounded. E-mail and MSN were about his limit. And what with the rules about turning off cell phones when in the lab, he usually forgot to turn his back on when he left.

He dialed her number. She picked it up after the first ring.

"Rafe?"

"Hi Tabby Cat! What's up?" he asked.

"Rafe," she said, her voice sounding serious. "Gammy's dead. She died this morning."

He didn't know what to say. His grandmother had treated him horribly after his First Shift, and he resented that tremendously. But he knew Tabitha had been very close to her.

"I'm...I'm sorry, Tabitha. How did it happen?"

"She was sitting in her chair, like normal, and mom gave her a nudge, like to wake her up. But she was dead. I think just old age." Her voice cracked as he told him. He knew she was struggling to keep it together.

"I think it's time you came home," she continued.

"Oh, Tabitha, I don't know. I've got a huge study which needs to be completed, and you know, Gammy and me, well..."

"This isn't for Gammy Rafe. This is for Mom. And for me. You need to be here for the funeral."

Rafe hesitated. He really didn't want to go back. He had put almost all of that part of his life behind him. On the other hand, he still felt guilty for abandoning Tabitha, and maybe it was time to see his mother and father again. He looked over at MJ, still engrossed in her work. Maybe a few days wouldn't hurt. He would clear it with Dr. Schilling, but yeah, maybe it was time.

"OK, Tabitha. Let me try to arrange it. When's the funeral?"

He could hear the sigh of relief on the other end of the phone. "Saturday, at 10:00 AM." There was a pause. "Thanks, big brother," she said softly. "Look, I gotta go. We've got lots of people here now. Send me a text when you think you'll arrive. Love you!"

He heard the connection cut off. "Love you too, Tabby Cat," he said softly into his dead phone.

He looked up at his girlfriend. "MJ, I need to take your car for a few days, OK?" Rafe had never owned a car, and MJ's Hyundai was a remnant of her marriage.

She finally broke her concentration. She looked up at him, her eyebrows scrunched together in a question. "Why?"

"My Gammy, I mean, my grandmother just died, and I need to go home for the funeral."

"But you have your isothermic studies due. You can't leave. You don't even contact your family anymore, so why go?"

"I have to. It's for Tabitha, more than anyone else. And I'll clear it with Dr. Schilling."

MJ shrugged. She had met Tabitha when she came to visit, and while there was no deep connection between the two, at least they had gotten along. "OK. It's up to you. I think you need to get your priorities straight, though." She immediately went back to work, the conversation in back of her.

That was his MJ, he thought, as he went over to put his arms around her neck, just standing there for a moment. She had a good heart, he knew. She just didn't know how to slot that heart into society's expectations. He gave her a gentle squeeze before letting go and going into the bedroom to pack a few things.

Chapter 20
the next day

Rafe was tired and a bit apprehensive as he drove down McCormick Avenue. He had driven all night, and for most of the night, he had worried about his reception. Driving past the old strip mall where he had done most of his shifts, he was somewhat disappointed to see that El Ranchito was no longer there. A Turkish restaurant had taken its place. Rafe hadn't been back for over 12 years, but he still felt a small pang of a lost youth.

The McDonald's was still there, going strong, but as he turned and drove past the house with the ever-protective Foo-foo, no little dog came out to challenge him. He slowly made his way up to the development. It looked the same as ever from the outside. He did notice some back-up spikes at the front gate, which were new, and there was security manning the gatehouse.

The guard didn't recognize Rafe's name, and no one had cleared him (he guessed he should have let Tabitha know he was close), but after a few calls were made, Rafe was waved through. He drove down the half-forgotten but still so familiar streets leading up to his home. In some ways, it seemed like he had never left, but in other ways, he could barely remember his life with the tribe.

There were a number of cars parked in the driveway and in front of his parent's house. He had to park a bit down the street. Leaving his backpack in the trunk, he locked the door and started to walk over. Standing on the porch was Tabitha, cell phone in her hand. She stood there waiting for him, one arm crossed in front of her chest holding her other elbow.

As he walked up, Rafe marveled again at how she had matured. Her childhood blondish curls had straightened and darkened to a chestnut brown, which still surprised him. But she had had also grown from a slightly pudgy, soft little girl into a slender, graceful young woman. She reminded him of Claire, and that brought a lump to his throat.

She waited until he reached the porch before throwing her arms around him.

"Thanks for coming, Rafe," she said, her voice catching a bit. She held him tightly, face buried in his chest. Finally, she released him from her hold and looked up at his face. "You ready for this?" she asked.

He took a deep breath, then simply answered "Yes."

Her arms slid from behind him as she shifted to his side, one arm migrating to hook his. She pushed open the door, and together, they stepped inside. There were a number of people sitting around, drinking coffee and speaking in muted tones. Rafe recognized most, but not all of them. Then he saw his mother, looking older, pouring coffee for Mrs. Simmons. At almost the same instant, his mother looked up and caught his eye. She paused for a second, questions forming as she saw Tabitha's arm still intertwined with his, then recognition dawned on her face. She gave a gasp, staggered, then put the coffee pot down before rushing across the room. She enveloped Rafe in a hug.

"Rafe! I didn't know...when did you...?" She looked over Rafe's shoulder as she hugged him at Tabitha. "You didn't tell me he was coming!"

Tabitha shrugged. "I wasn't sure he would go through with it, and well, you know, I didn't want to get anyone's hopes up."

"Oh, never mind." She pushed Rafe out at arm's length to look at him. "You've grown." She reached over and pushed a small lock of his hair back into place.

Rafe looked at his mother, and he felt guilty for the last 12 years. He realized that he loved her, and he missed her. While he could never live back with the tribe again, there was no reason that he had to cut off all contact. "I miss you, mom."

"Oh, I miss you, too. I am so glad you're home now, though." She suddenly turned around, hands still holding him as if he might disappear again if she let go. "Hank! Hank! Come here! Look who's back!" she called out.

Several of the people in the living room seem to suddenly recognize him. Fingers pointed as they told the others. Rafe couldn't help but notice a few frowns among them as they realized who he was.

His father came in, wiping his hands on an old towel. He looked up, and it took him only an instant to recognize his son. His eyes widened in surprise, and he strode across the room, hand out. More by instinct, Rafe took the hand and shook it. Whatever he had pictured about his reunion with his father, a formal handshake was not it. And that is not the way it ended. With a grunt, his father suddenly pulled him forward to throw an arm around him, hands slapping his back.

"Welcome home, son," he whispered in his ear.

The next few hours were rather awkward. Rafe was still dressed in sandals, Levis, and a USCD t-shirt, while the rest of the guests, those present when he came in and the seemingly never-ending stream of others, were in more formal wear. Some of the guests came up to welcome him back or give him their condolences: Mr. Peterson, Mr. and Mrs. Rodriguez, Mr. Kean, and a few others. Of his year group, only Lief seemed pleased to see him. Others either ignored him or went further to glare daggers at him. Trevor came over with Erica and two of their kids to pay their respects, and neither one of them would even catch his eye. One of their kids, though, a wide-eyed blonde boy of about three, kept his eyes on Rafe almost continuously. He wondered what the kid's parents had told him about him.

Finally, the last of the visitors left, and the four of them, with Jaifa still there, sat down to a light dinner. Rafe wasn't really in the mood to start going over his life story, and his parents seemed to sense it and left that topic alone.

Rafe had been ready to go check in the Motel 6 by the interstate, but his mother insisted that he stay in his old room. Reluctantly, and probably only because he still felt the guilt which had surfaced for not keeping in contact better, he agreed.

He went out to his car, moved it to the driveway, and took his bag out before coming back inside and climbing the stairs up to his old room. It really hadn't changed much in 12 years. Oh, there were none of the little personal bits of human detritus which indicated someone lived there, so it had a sterile feel, but the furniture and fittings were the same. He sat gingerly on the bed and after a moment, took a tentative bounce up and down. It felt the same.

With a sigh, he got up and started to take off his clothes to go take a shower. He had gotten his pants and shirt off and was about to take off his underwear when he stopped and chuckled. This wasn't his apartment with MJ and him alone in it. His parents and Tabitha were out there, and Jaira was staying full-time until after the funeral. He put his jeans back on, picked out a clean t-shirt and pair of shorts, and walked out to the small bathroom down the hall.

He paused outside of Tabitha's room and softly knocked on the door. There was no answer, so he opened the door a crack and looked in. The room had evolved from the little girl room he remembered to the young adult room it was now. Posters of two boy bands he didn't recognize and of Lady Gaga, who he did recognize, adorned the walls. No more My Little Pony or Barbie. He was about to close the door again when he caught sight of one toy on the nightstand by her bed. All alone, in a position of evident importance, was Remy. The stuffed blue rat looked a little worn for wear, but it was in surprisingly good condition for being almost 13 years old.

He was surprised to feel a little lump in his throat as he closed the door.

Jonathan P. Brazee

Chapter 21
the next afternoon

Rafe had to get out of there. Too many people were still stopping by, bringing covered dishes and condolences. And to him, too many people did not seem happy to see him. He told Tabitha he had to get out for a bit, then got into the Hyundai and drove out of the development. He didn't have a particular destination, but as he reached McCormick, it seemed that the car had a mind of its own as it pulled into the McDonalds.

Rafe didn't expect much after 12 years, but his pulse picked up a bit as he got out of the car and walked inside. He had never contacted Jenny after the night his sister was murdered, but he sometimes wondered how her life had gone.

"May I help you sir?" a very young girl asked him as he stood there. She couldn't have been more than 80 pounds soaking wet, and she looked much, much too young to be working to Rafe's 29-year-old eyes. Of course, Jenny was not there, nor did he really expect that.

"Oh, I'm sorry. Yea. Umm..., how about a Big Mac Meal?" Between Jaira's cooking and the food many of the guests were bringing, Rafe was not hungry, but he didn't want to look like an idiot, so he ordered the meal.

After ringing him up and assembling his meal, she gave him a cheerful "Thank you sir, come again!"

Sir? he thought. *I am too young to be a sir. And she is just too happy. Wait until life gets ahold of her.*

He took his meal to an empty table and started to eat it. He hadn't been to a McDonalds in quite awhile. MJ didn't approve of fast food, at least American fast food, although she loved those sodium-laced instant noodles. And there wasn't a McDonalds near the Scripps campus. So it was kind of nice to be tucking into a hot and greasy Big Mac.

He finished the Big Mac and went into the toilet to wash his hands before leaving. As he was passing through the door, a cheery "Come back soon, sir," followed him out.

He lifted one hand in a backwards wave in response, wanting to feel surly, but her cheerfulness was infectious. He was smiling as he got back in MJ's car. That smile died, though, as he drove past where Claire and he had been forced into the God's Judgment's car. Guilt swept over him. How could he have come here, ordered food, and eaten it without even thinking of Claire?

He drove down the road, but thinking of Claire, he had to stop and gather himself. He pulled into the strip mall where he had done his shifting and parked. He knew that life went on, that he had to get on with his life, but how could he have forgotten what happened last time he was at that McDonalds?

He got out of the car and started to walk around. He had usually been in at the mall at night, after the stores had closed. But now, the 10 or 15 stores were all open, and the place was surprisingly busy. His feet took him to the sidewalk in front of the stores and to the far end. Peering around the corner, he knew he had to see where he had first shifted on his own. He slowly sauntered down the side of the mall, and then in back. To his surprise, the huge dumpster was still in back. Nothing had changed, except for the smells of Turkish food rather than Mexican pervading the air. He wandered over to it and looked on the ground, right where he had shifted.

The rat stirred inside of him. Since Claire's murder, Rafe had never shifted. He refused, and he pushed his were so far down inside that it could not be sensed. He knew part of that was that his rat essence felt the guilt and felt unworthy of coming out. So his desires had been subsumed. They had been squeezed into a tight little ball and locked away forever.

For the first time in 12 years, his rat stirred, and in a panic Rafe pushed hard, pushed the rat back. He had to quell his desire.

Turning, he ran out of the alley, out and away from his temptation. He rounded the corner in a dead run and almost collided with a baby carriage being pushed by a rather large woman. She had two other kids in tow, and an older girl followed several paces in back of her.

"Sorry, sorry!" Rafe said as he danced, arms flailing as he tried to keep his balance and not fall into the stroller.

"Hey! Watch it!" the woman scolded him. She pulled the stroller back, then looked at Rafe with a puzzled expression.

"Rafe Turner? That's you, isn't it?" she asked.

Rafe had gotten his balance back and looked up at the woman. She was quite a large woman with perfectly coifed blonde hair. Her clothes looked a bit above the standard housewife fare. He had no idea who she was.

"Uh..., do I know you?" he asked.

"It's me. Jenny. Jenny Falkner. I mean, Jenny Smith before."

Something in her eyes and smile finally registered. "Oh my gosh! Jenny! I, well, I mean, it's great to see you again. Sorry I didn't recognize you for a moment." He hesitated and awkwardly made his way around the baby carriage to give her a hug and a kiss on the cheek. He had been thinking of Jenny back at the McDonalds, never expecting to see her again, and then he didn't even recognize her when he ran into her.

"Well, I know I've changed a lot since then." She spread her arms indicating herself, but Rafe didn't know if she meant her increased girth or the nicer clothes and accessories. "So where have you been? I never saw you again after that night, what, 11 or 12 years ago, the one where I met your sister. I called you a bunch of times, but your phone was off."

Rafe hesitated. He wasn't sure what to say. "Umm, that night, well, we had an accident. I was in an out-of-state university hospital for quite a long time, and when I recovered, well, I just started classes there." The lie flowed right off his tongue.

"Oh my gosh! I never knew! Are you all right now?"

"Sure. It took awhile, but I'm fine now."

"What about your sister? Was she hurt, too?"

Rafe didn't have to fake the pain when he replied, "She didn't make it. She died in the crash."

"Oh my gosh! Oh my gosh! I'm so sorry! I feel bad now. I was a little pissed at you when you didn't call, but if I had only known!"

The little boy holding her right hand looked up at Rafe with interest. He probably couldn't follow much yet, but he could sense his mom felt bad for Rafe.

Rafe did feel a bit guilty for concocting the story, but it wasn't that far from the truth, when you got down to it. He just preferred to leave the seedier aspects of his life after leaving private.

"This is actually my first time back since then. I came back for, I my grandmother's funeral."

"Oh, sorry about that. I keep saying 'sorry,' but I don't know what else to say."

Rafe wanted to change the subject. "So what about you?"

The tiny girl on her left looked up at her with arms raised. Jenny reached down and pulled her up to her hip.

"Well, as you can see, I'm married now, and a mommy."

"Yeah, wow, four kids."

"Actually six. It's one of those 'go forth and multiply' things. Dan and me—Dan's my husband—well, we take the Good Book seriously. That one back there," she jerked her thumb over her shoulder, "that's Grace. She's my second oldest. This young man is Joshua."

Joshua looked up and gave Rafe a surprisingly robust "Hi!"

"Hi to you, too, Joshua," Rafe responded.

"This little one is Anna," she told him, jiggling the little girl on her hip up and down, "and the baby is Simon. At home, I've got my oldest, Luke, and then my number three, Mark."

"Wow, six kids! I haven't even started yet!"

"You'll love it when you do. " She paused, obviously weighing if she should continue. Her need to speak won out. "You know, I always thought that you would have been my fist kiss."

"Mom!" Grace cried out.

"Hush. This is a long time ago." She turned back to Rafe. "Yes, I used to think about it, and I would come to work each day hoping you would come by. I guess I had a crush on you. But things work out for the best. If you and I had been a thing, I wouldn't have met Dan. I met him at MickyD's, too. About a month after you left, he started coming in, and well, you know how that goes."

"I'm glad things worked out for you."

Jenny didn't seem to want to stop. "Yeah, we fell in love while he was here in school. I had to keep working to keep us afloat. Then he got into grad school at Chicago." She put emphasis on the word to make sure Rafe realized the significance of that, which he actually did. The University of Chicago was a top-notch school. "So I worked at a MickyD's there to support us, even when my first two came along. Dan sometimes calls us the McFalkners," she said with a laugh, obviously an old family joke.

"So what do you do now?"

"Oh, I've served my last Quarter Pounder with Cheese. I'm a housewife now, and Dan was a VP for Mountain High Savings and Loan until he started his own bank last year. I guess you can say we do pretty well now." She held out her hand, which was adorned with a huge emerald ring. Rafe knew nothing about emeralds, but even to him, this one spelled "money."

"So we just bought a house on Osprey Lane, and ..."

"Mom, we've got to go! I need to get to class," Grace told her.

"Wait a minute, honey. I haven't seen Rafe here for years. Anyway, where was I?"

"Mom! I'm going to be late again!"

Jenny paused a moment, then sighed. "OK, OK. Get the little ones in the car."

Grace took the keys from her mother and started loading the younger kids into a new Volvo sedan. "Dan's got the Mercedes, as usual. Well, Rafe, it was great seeing you again. You really need to come over sometime to our place. It's not far from the Estate," she said, using the local nickname for the tribe's housing development. "I would love for you to meet Dan."

Grace started honking on the horn.

"Well, duty calls. Take my number and come give me a hug." She held out both arms, and Rafe dutifully moved forward to be enveloped by them. She gave him a sloppy kiss on the cheek, then let him go.

She gave him one last wave before getting into her car. Rafe watched her pull out of the parking lot before walking over and getting into MJ's Hyundai. Looking at his watch, he figured he should probably get back to his parent's house. He almost referred to it as getting back to his *home*, in his thoughts, but it wasn't his home anymore, nor had it been for quite some time.

Chapter 22
9:30 that evening

Dinner was rather informal that evening. Jaira didn't even cook as friends had brought over at least 15 covered dishes. Rafe grazed through most of them. A few were really quite dreadful, but several were out-and-out delicious. One lamb stew, with sort of a Middle Eastern flair, was superb. Rafe felt only a twinge of guilt as he helped himself to more than his share, cleaning out the casserole dish. This was something that should be on the Food Channel.

Thinking about the Food Channel, he looked back into the living room. His mother was sitting quietly on the big couch. The tv was off, and Rafe didn't feel he should waltz in and turn it on. It was still too early to go to bed, and he wasn't in the mood to work on his class study, so he walked over to give his mother a kiss on the top of her head before going out the front door.

It was still pretty warm as summer kept a lingering grasp on the land. In the distance, he could hear the drone of cicadas making the most of their brief life above ground. He couldn't tell one species of cicada from another by their songs, but it was likely that these had been living in the ground before Rafe left the tribe. And now that he was back, they emerged to sing in the night. At least he would like to think so, he thought to himself, a smile making a brief appearance on his face.

For the first time since he had returned, Rafe felt at ease with himself. He hadn't realized how much he missed his family, but being back reminded him of their love and care. He knew he couldn't live with the tribe on a permanent basis, but he really should have stayed in closer contact with his parents.

His feet took him wandering, his mind not really paying attention. He nodded to the few people he saw out and about, but as he was heading away from the community center, it got more and more isolated. He reached the end of Rosehip, which abutted the wall which surrounded the housing development section of tribal land. Over the wall was the Static world, his world now. It seemed pretty far away.

As he gazed over the wall at the treetops on the other side, a shadow moved behind him. He turned to see a large iron-grey wolf staring at him. His heart gave a small start, then calmed down almost immediately. Rafe knew that weres patrolled the perimeter now at night and had ever since Claire had been killed, so whomever this was, he or she was on guard duty.

The wolf shifted, and a few moments later, Trevor stood there, his gaze not wavering. He said nothing.

"Yes, Trevor, you want something?" Rafe felt a rise of something inside to him. Not a desire to shift. He hadn't had that in over 12 years. But a sense of trying to show dominance.

"You know, you've got a lot of balls coming back," Trevor finally said.

"Well, since my Grandmother died, I guess I can do what I want to support my family," he retorted.

"Your grandmother was a fine woman, but she knew what you were. What you are. And she wouldn't have wanted you to come back and dishonor her funeral."

"You don't know shit," retorted Rafe as he started to walk past Trevor.

Trevor shifted a couple of steps to intercept him. If he had been clothed, Rafe might have just brushed by him. But a naked man was somehow a more effective barrier.

"If you were any sort of a real were, your sister might still be alive with us. You killed her. And you killed the others, too."

Jonathan P. Brazee

Rafe inwardly winced. When he finally had gotten in touch with his sister, he was told that two weeks after Claire had been murdered, Rhett, Jorge, Jenifer, and a few older weres had travelled to the God's Judgment's compound in Kansas, without tribal approval, to extract revenge. No one ever heard from them since. He didn't reply to Trevor's accusation.

"Yea," Trevor nodded, "I see you know that. Even if your animal form is pathetic and useless, at least you were man enough to get the hell out of here, to leave the tribe."

He took a sudden step forward, almost bumping chests with the taller Rafe before Rafe took a quick step back.

"In deference to your family, no one's going to bother with you now. But after your grandmother's funeral, you gotta leave. We don't want you here, so go back to your jello world and rot, for all I care. You got that?"

Whatever sense of dominance Rafe had briefly felt a few moments ago had fled. He managed to dredge up a "I wouldn't dream of staying here any longer than I have to," but he was trembling as Trevor shifted back and left him standing there.

Chapter 23
Saturday morning

Rafe entered the tribal chapel with his parents and Tabitha. His grandmother was going to have two funerals: this one, for just tribe members, and one out in town at the Trinity Korean Pentecostal Church. His grandmother had been a long-time member of the church and had wanted to be buried in the church's cemetery.

His family filed into the front row which had been reserved for them. There was no casket being displayed as it was already at the church in town, but there was a lovely painting being displayed of a young version of his grandmother in traditional Korean clothes with a bear's head superimposed the sky above her. Rafe realized that while he had known his grandmother was a bear, he had never seen her in her bear form. On the lower corner of the painting was a small snapshot of the grandmother Rafe knew, looking so serious in a blue dress with her favorite pearls around her neck.

Mr. Sykes, Rhett's father, usually served as the tribe chaplain. He hadn't any formal religious training, as far as Rafe knew, but he tended to lead ceremonies such as this. Rafe figured that perhaps less than a third of the tribe had any dedicated religious leanings, but all seem to respect the idea of religion and those who were religious.

Mr. Sykes reached the pulpit and looked out over the packed pews. "We are here to honor JiYoung Sorenson, one of our tribe's most endearing members ...."

He went on to describe his Gammy's life, from her escape from North Korea through China to Thailand and back north to South Korea, her life alone as a young were awaiting her First Shift, her connecting with a South Korean tribe, her meeting a young American GI at a tribal function and on to her marrying that GI and coming with him to the US. Rafe's ears perked up a bit at this. He hadn't realized all the details of his Gammy's younger days. He knew she had been born in the north, but the rest of the story and how she had met his grandfather was all new to him.

Tabitha slid her arm around his and leaned into him. He snuck a quick glance at her to see her eyes moist. He gave her arm a squeeze.

Mr. Sykes finally sat down, and one after another, friends got up to speak their bits, to tell their Gammy stories. Rafe's mom had decided not to speak, so when the last friend sat down, Mr. Sykes retook the pulpit and led everyone in a generic prayer.

When he finished, he walked down the center aisle, followed by Rafe and his family. Outside the front door, they all stopped and took positions, ready to shake hands and listen to the condolences of all their friends.

Rafe barely put up with it. He kept wondering what was in back of those smiles, those handshakes, those words. They seemed earnest enough, but what were they really thinking? Finally, the last of them made it through their gauntlet. The family quickly walked out to the parking lot and got in his dad's Focus. If there wasn't yet to be a funeral out in town, they would all have gone to the community center for food. But as it was, time would be tight.

They got to the Korean church with about 10 minutes to spare. They quickly went inside and took the same places as they had at the tribal chapel. Only this time, in the front of the knave, was their grandmother's open casket. Rafe could see her face and folded hands across her chest. She seemed smaller than he remembered her. He felt most of the ill-will towards her he had harbored for the last 13 years fizzle away.

The pastor had evidently been awaiting their arrival, because after they sat down, the organ started up, and he stepped out from a passageway and up to the pulpit. After greeting everyone in English, he started going back and forth between English and Korean. And even in Korean, it had the same cadence and flow of the tribal funeral back at the chapel. One big difference, though, was that the service was interrupted several times for the singing of hymns.

Eventually, the service finished, and Rafe stood through a repeat of the hand shaking, condolence-giving line. A table had been set up, and some sort of sticky cakes were being served as well as what a lady serving drinks offered as tea. The tea tasted like burnt bread to Rafe.

Another older lady started herding the congregation to the cemetery on the side of the church. Gammy's grave site was evident with the hoist and flowers. They took their places around it and waited until the pallbearers made their appearance, eight men, including his father, carrying the closed casket. They solemnly placed the casket on the hoist, then stepped back. The pastor intoned a prayer in Korean while the casket was slowly lowered into the ground. Rafe's mom finally broke down into tears as the casket was halfway down, and that got Tabitha crying, too. They hugged each other, watching the casket make its final journey.

The pastor quit praying, then took a handful of dirt and threw it on the casket. Each person followed, throwing in one handful before leaving the cemetery and back to the church.

Rafe and his dad stood together, out of the flow of things while his mom made the rounds, At last, she came up to his dad and hugged him, telling him she was ready to go. The four of them got into the car and went home.

Chapter 24
that afternoon

Rafe finished stuffing his dirty shirts and underwear into his backpack. He thought about when he had left this same room so many years before. He wasn't carrying much more then than he was now. But maybe he should plan on keeping in better touch from now on.

With one last glance around the room, he slowly closed the door behind him and walked down the hallway. It had an air of being deserted, despite the fact that his mother, father, and Tabitha still lived there.

Walking down the stairs, he could hear quiet movement in the kitchen. Jaira was undoubtedly trying to clean up. He was ready to leave, to get back home and to MJ, and he didn't feel like getting into a drawn-out conversation with Jaira, so he took a seat on the overstuffed couch. Looking over to his left was Gammy's rosewood chair, the same chair from which she stood sentinel on the family for so many years. He shrugged. Now, it was just a chair to him.

He checked his watch. Tabitha was probably going to run late. She had left with some friends to visit Gammy's grave. None of the friends had wanted to go to a Static church for the ceremony, and he thought Tabitha wanted a bit of time at the grave with her friend's support. Rafe really wanted to get on the road, but he was not going to leave without saying goodbye to her.

He was texting a message to MJ telling her he was about to leave when a hand touched his shoulder. He jumped in startlement before looking up and seeing it was his mother. Her eyeliner was still a bit smeared from earlier tears, but she looked composed.

"I want to thank you for coming back. Your dad and me, well, we miss you, and while we know you are OK, it is still good to see our baby. " She moved around the side of the couch and sat down beside him.

"I know you and mom had issues since, well, you know, but she still loved you. She just had a way about her, and she was very traditional, you know. But she would have been happy that you came home for this."

Rafe didn't say anything. He doubted very much that his grandmother would have wanted him there, but he came for his mother, his father, and of course, for Tabitha. Not for his Gammy. It just wasn't worth it to take issue with his mother's view. He accepted her arm as it came around his. They sat there in silence, a grieving mother and her supporting son. He heard a soft sniffle and looked down to see the tears had started again, making new tracks of eyeliner coming down her cheeks.

They sat there in silence for a few minutes, the only sounds being the quiet clatter of dishes being put away in the kitchen and the soft ticking of the old grandfather clock in the entranceway. Rafe knew his mother needed his presence, but he was getting anxious to get going, to get back to his real life. He tried a surreptitious glance at his watch, but his wrist was buried in this mother's grasping arms.

A sudden buzzing could be heard in from the dining room, which was followed by *Ode to Joy*. "Oh, that's mine. Let it ring for once," she told him.

After a few moments, the phone mercifully turned off, but the respite was short-lived. Almost immediately, the buzzing could be heard again, then Beethoven once again reached them, seeming anxious for attention.

"Goodness! Can't they leave me alone for once?" she asked in exasperation.

When the phone started it third set of ringing, his mother untwined her arms from Rafe's and got up, muttering as she walked into the dining room and her phone. Rafe absently listened to her "Hello?" as he settled back down into the couch.

"What? When?" his mother's frantic voice caught his full attention. "Are you sure?" Rafe sat up straight, looking back over the couch and into the dining room.

"I'm coming right now," his mother said with urgency. Then she shouted out "Hank! Come here now!"

Rafe stood up as his mother came back into the living room. Her eyes were wide as she looked at him. "They've got Tabitha!"

Chapter 25

Rafe rushed into the community center with this mother and father.   Half-a-dozen others were already there, all surrounding an obviously shaken young man who Rafe vaguely recognized as one of Tabitha's friends. He was sitting down, in obvious pain. He looked like he was about to pass out.

The others looked up as the three of them rushed up and then parted for them, letting them get right up to the guy.

"OK, Jarrod, Tabitha's mom and dad are here. Tell them what you just told us," Hector Manuel told him.

Jarrod looked up at them, wringing his hands together. It was only then that Rafe noticed a bright red burn mark around his right wrist. Eric, the manager of the community center was holding a huge pair of cutters in hands, and he was using it like a curling broom to push a bent and cut silver bracelet-looking thing to the side of the room and into a trashcan being held by a young woman Rafe didn't recognize. The band was about the same size as the burn on Jarrod's wrist, so it was pretty obvious that Eric had just cut it off him.

"Mr. Turner, I couldn't do anything about it. They put that silver band on me before I could shift, and they...."

"Jarrod, slow down! What happened? Where's Tabitha?" asked his father, tension evident in his voice as he tried to control himself.

"They took her and Katie."

"Who took her, and took her where?" his mother asked.

Just then several more people rushed in. One woman rushed to Rafe's mother.

"Bill's on his way. What's happened?" she asked in a panicky voice.

"Someone's got Katie and Tabitha. Jarrod was with them, and we're trying to find out what happened."

"Oh God!" the woman cried out, stumbling in his mother's grasp until someone hurriedly pushed over a chair in which she could collapse.

Jarrod seemed to zone out for a moment. His eyes rolled up and he started to collapse in the chair.

"No, not now, Jarrod! We need you here!" Manuel cried out, shaking the young man's shoulder.

Jarrod seemed to get ahold of himself, and with an obvious effort, sat up straighter in the chair. "Sorry, sorry. I know. I'm just feeling real bad right now. I think I'm going to throw up."

Rafe's father grabbed Jarrod by both arms, interrupting the young man. "Jarrod. I need to know. What happened?"

Jarrod took a deep breath before answering. "We went to see Tabitha's grandmother's grave, like alone, without all the jellos there. I drove them so her and Katie could be there."

The sitting woman, obviously Katie's mother, gasped.

"Then these people came up, and ..."

"What people?" blurted out Rafe's father.

Manuel put his hand on Rafe's father's shoulder. "Let him tell us, Hank," he said softly, understanding in his eyes.

"God's Judgment. That's who they said they were."

Rafe felt the world closing in on him. God's Judgment? The same group who took his older sister from him now had his younger? He felt the anger begin to bubble up inside of him. He lost track for a moment of what Jarrod was saying, and he had to focus to get back into the situation.

"...and after they hit me on the head, when I was sort of out of it, that's when they slapped that bracelet-thing on me. It hurt like a bitch, and that cleared my head real fast. I wanted to shift and take their throats out, but I couldn't. And I could see Katie and Tab being dragged away. They had silver, like, blankets or something on their heads, and they were pushed into a van. I could hear them screaming. I wanted to do something, but I couldn't."

"You couldn't because they put that silver thing on you to keep you from shifting?" asked a voice from the growing crowd.

"Yeah, I think so. My head was fucked up...oh sorry, my head was screwed up, and my arm was on fire, and when I could think again, I couldn't shift. Then their leader, I guess, he comes up to me and says to go back and tell you all here that God's Judgment's got Katie and Tabitha. He says his name is Anton Borisov, and we should remember that name."

Rafe started. "Was he a thin guy with dark hair?"

"Well, yeah, he was."

Rafe felt the pit of his stomach sink. He knew that guy. "He was the one who killed Claire" was all he said.

Gasps and cries of outrage surrounded him. He tuned them all out. This was the fucker who killed his sister. And now he had his younger sister. His stewed in a combination of rage and guilt while others milled about, trying to digest what had happened.

Katie's father made it to the community center and had to be brought up to speed. Others gathered in groups trying to decide what to do. One young woman, Telly, Rafe thought her name was, came back with a large print of the God's Judgment compound, thanks to Google Earth. From the satellite view, the compound looked something like an old-time castle. The large open area in the middle was surrounded on all four sides with walls, but walls thick enough to house living areas, offices, or whatever. The open area had what looked to be a parking area, a basketball court, and an open expanse of grass. Towards the back of the compound, up against the back wall, was a good-sized chapel. A few yards to the side was a small outbuilding. People began to pour over the map. No one in the tribe had ever served in the military, but enough arrows and symbols soon sprouted up on the map to make the D-Day plan look inadequate.

Someone soon suggested going to the Static police, a suggestion quickly shouted down by the others. This was their problem, one they would fix themselves.

All the while, Rafe sat quietly amidst the uproar. He took out his cell and texted MJ, letting her know he would be delayed in coming home. He may have failed Claire, but somehow, he was not going to fail his Tabby Cat.

Chapter 26
early the next day

"OK, then, everyone got it? I want everyone to get a few hours rest. We're going to need it. Let's meet back here at ...," Greg Sykes, who had taken over the gathering, looked at his watch for a moment. "...2:00 PM. I want to be moving out no more than 30 minutes later. We've got a long drive ahead of us. Be back here sharp with the gear you've been assigned."

The crowd began to break up as people made their way over the crushed coffee cups and McDonalds wrappers littering the floor of the community center. Rafe stood up from where he had been sitting quietly during the often contentious planning for the rescue. He made his way up to Sykes, pulling on his arm.

"And what about me, Greg?" he asked once he had his attention. It felt weird calling him "Greg" rather than the "Mr. Sykes" he had always previously used, but Rafe figured he was now an adult, and he wanted to stress to him that he was a full member of the tribe and on equal footing. "Mr. Sykes" would make him sound like he was still the young boy who had fled so many years before.

"Tabitha's my sister, and I'm involved, like it or not."

To his credit, Greg did not flippantly dismiss him. He paused for a moment. "Well, Rafe, I know you're worried, and I know you want to help, but you've heard the plan, and well, well, I'm not sure how you really can help? I mean, you can't really fight, can you? And do some good? Maybe you should stay here and help Angie cope. That'd be pretty helpful."

Angie was Angie Kellerman, Katie's mother. She hadn't been able to take the stress and had been taken home some hours ago.

"You didn't hear me, Greg." He put as forceful of an emphasis as possible on the "Greg." "I'm coming, and that is that. You tell me where you want me, or I'm leaving for their compound right now on my own."

Greg looked hard into Rafe's eyes, seeing the fierce determination reflected back at him. He grudgingly nodded his acceptance.

"OK. Tell you what. You drive the second van. You remember what your task is for that?"

Rafe merely nodded.

"I'll tell Maria, and that will give me one more eye in the sky after the recon, 'cause she can just stay on station rather than come back to the van." He slapped Rafe's shoulder. "All OK?"

Rafe thought for a second. He wanted something more, well, heroic, but at least he would be contributing. And the girls would be going back in his van after being rescued.

"Thanks, Greg."

Both men nodded at each other before Rafe turned around and left the building. He didn't think he could get any sleep, but he knew he had to try. He had to be ready to do his part.

Chapter 27
late the next afternoon

The caravan pulled into the city park at the edge of town. Each vehicle pulled into a parking spot towards the rest rooms on the gently sloping bank which led to a small lake. An old man, probably in his 80's, was fishing on the near shore. He didn't look up as the members of the rescue team piled out, at least half heading for the rest rooms. The rest stood and stretched before slowly gathering around the lead Escalade.

A shepherd mix came bounding out of the trees at the edge of the parking lot, barking furiously. The tribe members merely looked at the brave mutt, some acknowledging its spirit. But they didn't really want to be attracting attention, so Sandy Poorhouse took a few quick steps toward the dog as if in attack mode. The dog turned tail and ran, but only for about 10 or 15 yards before it turned back to face them and commence barking again. Sandy had to make a more concerted dash at the dog before it finally gave up and fled through the trees.

It took a few minutes for everyone to return from the rest rooms, and as they all gathered around Greg, the tension ratcheted up one more level.

"Are we all here?" Greg started counting heads. "Tank, your attention please?"

Tank Sherman had been suspiciously watching the old fisherman, but he sheepishly turned his attention back to the group. Rafer realized that he didn't even know Tank's real name. He had always just been "Tank," a reference to both his stocky build and his last name. In a poetic world, Tank would be a werebear or maybe even a rhino, but no, he was a red-tailed hawk.

"OK, Tank, Maria, and Alysha, get ready. Remember what you're supposed to be looking for. We'll wait here until you report back."

All three nodded and went to the back of the Winnebago, shucking off their clothes even before getting in the back. But with all the others surrounding them, Rafe figured no one could see them.

Alysha had actually married outside of the tribe to a guy from the Austin Tribe, but she had been visiting home with her new baby girl when Tabitha and Katie were taken, so she insisted on helping out. Her husband (Rafe never caught his name) was also eager to help.

All three of them piled into the back of the Winnebago and dropped their clothes. Tank kissed his tribal medallion, almost like people kissing a rosary, then the three of them shifted. The raptors flew out, their cries piercing the air, wings laboriously beating as they gained altitude. The two hawks were quicker than the golden eagle, but soon, all three were lost to sight.

"And now we wait," said Greg to no one in particular.

In military operations, soldiers might be cleaning weapons, loading ammunition, or getting whatever armored vehicles ready for action. But for the tribe, their bodies were the weapons. None of them had opposable thumbs in their were mode, so most hand weapons were useless, even if there wasn't a cultural bias amongst the tribe on using such. They had brought a sledgehammer, a blowtorch, and some rope to be used while in human form, and these could be strapped onto their were forms to be used when needed. They could simply shift back to use them. But none of these really needed to be checked over and over again, not that that stopped them from doing so out of sheer nerves. Even medallions, which were essentially foolproof, were turned on and off to make sure they worked.

Rafe wasn't even in the assault team, but he still felt those nerves. Maybe it would be better if he was facing direct violence. Then things would be in his own hands, at least to an extent. But as a glorified bus driver, he had no real impact on the events which would be unfolding.

For lack of anything better to do, he wandered down to the lakeshore. The old man was still there, almost motionless as he watched a bright red and white bobber float a few yards offshore. Tall and thin, Rafe wondered how he managed to stand so still. It seemed as if a stiff breeze would blow him over. His face was a roadmap of long, tough years, his neck a waddled patchwork of folded skin. He had on a faded mostly red flannel shirt and overalls. A well-worn Pioneer Hi-Bred ballcap covered his hair. The only thing taking away from the redneck attire was the pair of lime green flipflops on his feet.

"You uns in a gang or sumptin?"

It took Rafe a moment to realize that the creaky voice coming from the oldster was directed at him.

"What?" he asked stupidly.

"A gang. You don have no motorcycles, but you got the feel of a gang."

"Ah, no. We're just passing through," he stammered out.

The man cracked his neck to the side ever so slightly, to look at Rafe out of the corner of his eye. "Nah, you're a gang. I knows it," he intoned with a degree of finality. He turned his head back forward to look at his bobber.

Rafe knew he had been dismissed. Obediently, although he wasn't sure why, he turned and walked back up to the group. Most had broken up into small subgroups where they discussed football, food, television—anything but the upcoming rescue. Rafe wasn't part of them, and he knew it. He went back into his assigned van and sat in the driver's seat. Better to wait it out here than with anyone else.

Lost in his thoughts, he didn't notice the return of the raptors. Only the commotion outside caught his notice, and he got out of the van to see two of the three raptors back in human form. Someone had thrown each of them a robe, which they now wore as they briefed Greg and the rest. Alysha, with the best soaring ability and eyes, had remained over the compound. She couldn't see as well at night, but it was still better to have someone high overhead during the rescue.

None of them had seen any evidence on exactly where the girls were being held, so the plan was to go with their initial assumption that they would be in the outbuilding beside the chapel. Rafe wasn't quite sure how the group had come up with that assumption, but it seemed as logical as any. It would be easier to control that building than any of the conjoined rooms within the compound's surrounding walls. And if they weren't there, then, well, things would have to be improvised.

The sharp-eyed scouts had found three armed guards: one making rounds on the flat roof of the building, one each in the compound's two watch towers. There was very little activity in the open areas, which seemed a bit strange, and no dogs, which seemed even stranger. But the fewer people with which to deal, the better.

Greg went over the plan, such as it was, one more time. The overall tactic was to make this a bum rush, each in their animal form. They would enter the high gateway going through the front wall, and then most of the team would spread out through the compound, wrecking havoc (and taking revenge) on whomever they found. The "strike force," as Greg christened it, would head straight for the outbuilding and rescue the girls. Both of Rafe's parents were on the team, as was Greg, Rob Goodpastor, Bill Kellerman (Katie's father), and Shelly Angeles, a werepuma a few years older than Rafe. Rafe didn't know Shelly well, but evidently, she was quite a fierce were. She was also Katie's sister. Greg was to take the human form in case the blowtorch needed to be used to free the girls.

Rafe was a little uneasy that both his parents would be on the strike force, but his mom was probably the most deadly were in the tribe, and he knew his dad was not going to be left behind.

What to do with any church member who did not put up any resistance was an uneasy and unspoken dilemma. There were families there, children. These children might grow up to be the tribe's mortal enemies someday, but could they morally be killed at this stage? No one spoke about it, and probably most of the team didn't know yet what they would do when faced with the situation.

"OK, any last minute questions?" asked Greg to the group. When no one responded, he continued, "I want to remind you that this is more than just our two girls. These bastards are our mortal enemies, make no bones about it. And it's time to extract some revenge. Don't do anything stupid. We need all of you back. But don't give these fuckers any mercy."

It may not go down as one of the most memorable pre-fight speeches, but the group yelled out their approval. Even Rafe joined in the mindless shout.

"OK! Let's get rolling! We know what we've got to do now," Greg directed them.

There was a hustle as the 30 plus weres, all ready for battle, rushed to cram into the vehicles. Rafe started the big Chevy's engine, then pulled in back of the Escalade. His was to be the second vehicle in. As the Escalade pulled out of the parking lot, Rafe followed, anxiety rising. He wanted to floor the accelerator, to rush to Tabitha's rescue. But despite the four cars and one Winnebago being normal vehicles to be seen on the street, they needed to stay under the radar of the local authorities. So blood pumping, hands clenched into the steering wheels, they drove at a plodding 30 MPH out of town and down the country highway towards their enemy's lair in the darkening evening.

After a slow 40 minutes, and as the Escalade turned left and down the narrow road leading up to the compound, Rafe hung back a bit. They didn't want to look like an obvious convoy, so the idea was to get a bit of room between them, then the trailing cars would speed up so they could all arrive together. He turned off his headlights, trusting his driving ability to keep the van on the road. They proceeded for another 5 or 10 minutes. Time was blurring, so Rafe was not sure just how long he drove.

"You are 500 yards from your destination," the polite female voice on the van's GPS finally informed him.

"OK, guys, get ready," he told his passengers. They started taking off their clothes, to be ready at a moment. They wouldn't shift until actually outside the van, though.

Rafe sped up. The van bounced along the dirt road, throwing his passengers in the back around. He didn't notice. All he wanted to do was to arrive at the same time as the lead vehicle.

That vehicle's bright red brake lights flared. Rafe hadn't realized he was so close given the darkness, but he swerved to the side and slammed to a stop. Immediately, the people in the back jumped out the back door and shifted, medallion lights glowing like fireflies. Another van and the Winnebago pulled up alongside of the Chevy, and in moments, there was a rise in energy, almost palpable as people shifted to wolves, bears, coyotes, a puma, a hyena, and one very angry tiger. Rafe looked over and caught Maria's eye. She had switched to driving the other van, freeing up that driver, Saul, to take his place with the team. With the darkness, there was not much she could do, and a coyote would offer the team more firepower, so-to-speak.

There was an amorphous sense of movement, almost like the incoming tide, and the weres pushed forward, waiting for Greg to start the charge. The driver of the Caddy, a young man whose name never registered with Rafe, finished strapping on the blowtorch and sledgehammer to the big werebear's back. Greg looked back, then with a roar, started his lumbering charge. Immediately the air was filled with howls and more roars as the group started forward, and unstoppable force, a bigger force than had ever gathered in anyone's memory.

Expecting some resistance, if they were surprised that the entrance going through the front wall seemed abandoned, they never showed it. The ground at the entrance was covered in what looked like to Rafe as a thick canvas, like an Army surplus tent. In his eagerness, Rafe stepped forward to get a better look, despite the fact that he had been told to stand by his van in order to make a speedy getaway. The entrance was basically an opening wider than Rafe expected (although in retrospect, it would have to be wide to allow trucks and such to enter) and reaching from the ground to the roof overhead, giving a large enough field of vision to take in most of the inner compound. The lights of the compound were on, making the rushing weres stand out as the rushed across the huge grassy courtyard. It was an impressive sight, and Rafe felt a sense of pride filling him. These bastards were going to pay, and pay dearly for what they had done.

He only peripherally caught the movement at the gate as the canvas-like ground cover seemed to be jerked back, revealing a gleaming silver ramp leading into the compounds proper. This looked like real metal. Rafe looked at that in puzzlement for a second as the first shots rang out. Immediately, more shots rang out, automatic gunfire coming from windows surrounding the open courtyard.

With a start, Rafe realized in an instant that God's Judgment had been lying in wait. He rushed forward instinctively, not really thinking what he could do. He could see inside the compound better now, and the sight made him sick. Several weres were down, and they looked to be down hard. Normal bullets were problematic, but even a few bullets should not hold a were down unless it was a killing shot, and weres were pretty tough. A werebear rushed the wall of the side building, obviously preparing to climb it to get at their attackers. As he or she reached up and touched the wall, the werebear immediately fell back to the ground in obvious pain. It was only then that Rafe really accepted the power of the silver solution used on the wall. Rounds then pounded the bear, each round causing a small, visible disturbance in the bear's shaggy coat until it lay still. Rafe didn't know if they were silver or lead rounds, but they certainly were effective.

Panic gripped Rafe. He rushed forward to the edge of the silver ramp. A wolf made a run for the gateway, but as it stepped on the other side of the ramp, it howled in agony and fell, its body laying on the bare silver. Rafe imagined he could hear the werewolf's fur sizzling. Without thinking, he rushed out onto the ramp and grabbed the wolf by the tail. Rushing back, he literally pulled the wolf out of the compound and fell with it to the naked ground. A few rounds seem to follow them out, but none hit close to them.

Maria, the young Escalade driver, and Chet Craig, the Winnebago driver rushed over to help. The wolf was out of it, but breathing. Rafe wondered how he had been able to walk on the ramp. Then it hit him. In his panic, he had forgotten his hiking boots, he looked down at them. Their thick soles had kept him from direct contact with the terrible metal.

"You guys, come with me!" he shouted at the others. As they rushed back up the gate, a coyote at full speed came barreling towards the ramp. It managed to take a few extra bounds before collapsing, but its momentum carried him past the lip of the ramp and onto the bare ground.

The firing had slacked off a bit, but Rafe could see the carnage in the courtyard. Several weres had already gathered at the edge of the ramp, desperately seeking a way out. A large wolf shifted, and Trevor stood there. He put one foot tentatively on the ramp, then cried out in pain. Rafe rushed over the ramp, and as a round hit another wolf there, he yelled out for Trevor to get on his back.

Trevor looked down at the shoes, then quickly realized what had to be done. He jumped on Rafe's back and rode piggyback to the naked dirt outside the gate. The other drivers had also gotten into position to piggy back a few others to safety, but others weren't changing as Rafe rushed back forward. He yelled at them to change, but then noticed the bloody holes in a few.

Being shot by silver bullets in non-vital areas might not kill a were right away, but it stopped them from being able to shift and would probably soon render him or her unconscious. Rafe reached down and picked up a huge wolf, hoisting him over his shoulder. Rounds pinged around him as he ran back out the gate. Someone had obviously reloaded during the brief lull.

Trevor, still naked, but with shoes on, rushed back into the compound, shouting instructions. Those weres that could began to gather closer to the gateway, taking whatever cover they could.

There was a rush and something huge flew through the air past Rafe as he struggled with another large wolf. He looked out to see his mother had completely cleared the 30 feet or so of silver. She looked unhurt but terribly angry.

Finally, despite the now sporadic fire, a voice called out to get back into the vehicles. It wasn't Greg's voice, though. Rafe looked around. Greg wasn't there. There was no one else waiting to be ferried over the silver. All that could make it had done so. He edged to the side of the long gateway, looking inside the compound. He could see half-a-dozen bodies right in his line of sight. They weren't moving.

A door to one of the buildings opened up, and a familiar figure came out. Rafe hadn't seen him for 12 years, and the man was a good 30 or 40 yards away, but he immediately recognized him. Anton Borisov.

Anton systematically walked up to each downed were and shot each one in the head to the cheers of the unseen men and women still manning the guns. Anton looked to the gateway and seemed to catch Rafe's eyes. He smiled, and aimed his handgun at him, then brought it down, mimicking blowing way smoke as in the old westerns.

"Come on, we've got to go." Trevor grabbed him by his arm, pulling him back. "We've got people who need help."

"But, but what about them?" Rafe asked, indicating the compound behind him.

"We can't help them anymore. No one can. And we need to get out of here now. But believe me, those fuckers are going to pay." Anger almost flared out of Trevor's eyes.

"Now, I said!" he bellowed out as he turned to look at the others. "Get in the fucking cars now!" The shell-shocked people, both in human and animal form, started loading the vehicles.

"You too, you asshole," he shouted at Rafe, pushing him forward.

Rafe went unresisting, his mind in a daze. He hadn't seen his father, didn't even know who had made it and who hadn't. But he got into the now only partially full van and drove off into the night and safety.

Chapter 28
back at the tribe the next day

It was a weary and dispirited group which gathered back at the tribal community center. Trevor and a few others were briefing the rest of the gathered tribe members on what had happened. Looks of disbelief seemed to be the order of the day.

Thirty-seven weres had left on the rescue. Twenty-nine had returned. The weres in the last van had never even made it to the God's Judgment compound. In the darkness, their driver had gone off the road and gotten stuck. That van's weres had left the vehicle in the ditch and were running to the compound when they met the retreating rescue party. Tank Sherman caught up with them there as they spread themselves out into the remaining vehicles.

Greg Sykes hadn't made it. Rafe hadn't seen him go down, but evidently, his head had been completely blown off his large body. The bastards must have had at least one very large caliber weapon to do that.

Gael Herman, a coyote a year older than Rafe had been killed, as had his sister, Lorissa, a wolf. Rafe knew Gael quite well and rather liked him. He knew the older Lorissa, of course, but not as well.

Three other wolves had not made it as well: Fanny Steptoe, John Santos, and Justin Pavoni. All were his parent's age. Justin and his family had often been guests for Sunday BBQ's at the Turner house, and Rafe had warm memories of the funny, laughter-filled man.

Tom Amirault, Alysha's husband, had not made it either. He was the bear who had tried to scale the wall to get at their attackers. He wasn't even a member of the tribe, but he had willingly gone into battle for them.

To make matters worse, Alysha hadn't been seen since the attack. No one knew if she had been killed or not, but most feared the worse.

Most of the others had healed or were close to it by the time they reached the tribe's own gate. They had stopped shortly after getting back on the main highway, and with either their own bodies pushing out the rounds, or with the assistance of sharp knives wielded by others, the silver bullets were expelled, taking away the immediate pain even if the lingering effects kept them from shifting. Three weres, though, one of them being Lief, were unconscious, the silver bullet too deep or fragmented to be pulled out. These three had been rushed to the small nursing station in the community center the moment the rescue party returned.

Some injuries, though, were not physically apparent. Rafe glanced over at his father. The man seemed diminished, a shadow of his former self. Once a major figure in the tribe, he had seemingly relinquished any position of authority. Losing Tabitha opened old wounds, and the subsequent death of more weres, especially his close friends Greg and Justin, had taken their toll on him. He sat slumped over in a seat in back of the main group, dejection apparent in every aspect of his body. To see him like that tore Rafe apart.

The voices of the others got louder and more stringent. Rafe turned his attention from his father and back to the main group.

"It's too late. I've already contacted the United Tribes," Mr. Peterson said firmly. Adult now or not, Rafe didn't feel comfortable referring to him as anything other than "Mr. Peterson."

"But this or our problem, and we're going to solve it!" shouted back Trevor.

"Like you just did? Getting eight of us killed?" Mr. Peterson asked calmly.

Trevor's face broke out into a rage. "How dare you?" he shouted again before his features began to flow. Within moments, his wolf stood there covered in the torn remains of his clothes, a deep growl emanating deep from within his throat. He took a step forward.

Mr. Peterson merely looked down at the angry wolf. "Do you really think that's going to change anything?" he asked dismissively.

Several others reached over to pull Trevor back. Erica put her arms around his neck and whispered into his ear. It took a few moments, but the Trevor the wolf calmed down and shifted back. Trevor the man stood there in his tattered clothing, still glaring, but all human now.

"Now, as I was saying,..." Mr. Peterson went on, as if a full-grown werewolf hadn't just been ready to tear out his throat. "... the United Tribes have been brought up to speed. They are sending in someone to investigate and help. They've asked us not to do anything until he arrives. He's on the plane now, and he should be here by evening."

There was shifting of weight and some low grumbling, but no one said anything.

"We're all pretty worked up right now. I would suggest that we all go to our homes for awhile, take a hot bath or whatever. Let's meet back here at 8:00 PM. OK?" Mr. Peterson looked around at the others.

No one seemed happy about breaking things up yet. They wanted to take action, the sooner the better. But Mr. Peterson was right. The crowd slowly started to break up.

Rafe went over to his father. "Come on, Dad. Let's get home."

His father looked up at him with a blank expression on his face. He didn't get up.

"Let's go home, Hank," his mother said to his father as she came up alongside Rafe.

Together, they got his father to his feet and started the walk home. Some people strode angrily by, fueled by anger. Others stumbled along like his father, more in shock than anything else. It took longer than normal, but they finally got home. Rafe helped his mother get his father up the stairs and into their bedroom.

"Thanks, Rafe," his mother simply said as they lay his father back in the bed, on top of the bedspread.

Rafe nodded and left them there. Going back to his room, he paused outside Tabitha's room. Hesitating, he knocked softly on the door, as if maybe she had been in there all along, that this had all been a dream. Shaking his head in self-embarrassment for knocking, he opened the room. It was quiet and musty, almost as if no one had ever lived there.

In his place at the nightstand at the head of the bed stood Remy, looking out at him. Rafe walked over and picked him up. Remy stared benignly back. What was in that stuffed little head, wondered Rafe.

Keeping his hold on the stuffed toy, he turned around and left, carefully closing the door behind him. He got to his own room and lay down on the bed. Holding the blue rat close, he surprisingly drifted off to sleep.

Chapter 29
8:00 PM at the community center

Rafe felt surprisingly refreshed as he sat in the corner, drinking his coffee. People drifted around in small groups, dissolving and reforming in different combinations as they wondered who was coming. Mr. Peterson and Chet Craig had left to go to the airport, and they were expected to return with their guest any minute.

"Doesn't really matter who they send. This is our tribe, and it's up to us to deal with it as we please," Tank's voice cut through the general murmurs of twenty different conversations.

"Damn straight." Trevor's voice agreed.

Rafe wondered if that was true. Technically, each tribe was a separate entity, bowing to no one else. But still, the United Tribes held sway, with the mysterious council taking action when needed. Fortunately, it was rarely needed. Rafe had never given the council much thought one way or the other.

He took another sip of his coffee. He had never really liked coffee, only drinking it when he lived on the street. But MJ had showed him a different side to the brew, and now he appreciated the various blends and flavors. This coffee wasn't bad, he thought. And then felt guilty for noticing such a mundane thing when the tribe's world was falling apart.

Just then, Mr. Peterson and Chet came in the door, followed by a small, trim man. Balding, standing at about 5'6", and maybe tipping the scales at 150 pounds, he didn't overtly look very impressive, that was for sure. But he did move with a sense of purpose and strength. Despite his innocuous appearance, Rafe was sure this man knew what he was doing.

Mr. Peterson got to the podium at the front of the room and called out, "Can I have everyone's attention please?" And the room quieted down and looked towards him, he continued, "I have here Colonel Joshua Hartigan. He just arrived to assess the situation and offer his assistance. He's going to need a bit of time to be brought up to speed, but he's got a few words to say now." He looked at the small man. "Colonel?"

"Thank you, Sean," he said as he stepped up to the podium. He adjusted the mic down to his level. "As Sean told you, I'm Josh Hartigan. And I'm here to tell you that you screwed up, plain and simple."

The crowd exploded into protests. Colonel Hartigan simply held up one hand until most of the uproar subsided, ignoring some pointed remarks thrown his way.

"It's not really your fault, though. Over the last 100 years or more, we've knocked the fight out of ourselves. We are not our great-grandfather's weres. We want to coexist with our cousins, not feed on them. Yes, that's probably a good thing, but our cousins are still the barbaric killers who first came down out of the trees. While we have embraced the Kingdom of Kumbaya, they've killed Jews, Armenians, Tutsis, Khmers, Sunnis, Shia, and you name it by the millions. And some of them still want to exterminate us." He paused to let all that sink in.

"Now I've been sent here to assess things. If appropriate, and only if I approve, yes, we will take action against God's Judgment." You could hear the venom in his voice as he said the name. "And if I decide, your tribe can mete out the punishment. But only if I decide."

"And who the fuck are you to tell us what we can or can't do? We can handle this ourselves," shouted Trevor as he stepped forward to confront the colonel. There were murmurs of agreement from most of the rest.

"You can handle it?" the colonel answered back, a sneer on his face. "Like you handled it enough to get eight people killed?"

Trevor lunged forward, starting to shift again. An involuntary shift due to anger was rare among weres, and this was twice in less than 24 hours for him. But then again, things were highly agitated.

"Stop!" the colonel ordered, with enough snap of authority in his voice that Trevor did stop, to Rafe's surprise. "You want to take me on? Well fine. We'll see to that later. And I'll show you that a thinking human, in human form, can defeat any werewolf, hand-to-hand. It's your anger that clouds you into forgetting that were or not, you are human. And humans' asset is their brain. You all thought that just by shifting, you could defeat any group of people. Didn't work out to well, did it? Let me tell you young man, even keeping my human form, make no mistake that you could not take me."

"How about me?" asked Patty Vander Horst.

"And your were form?"

"A bear," she said with satisfaction.

"Hand to hand, no. I couldn't. But being a human means that I know where and how to fight. I know enough not to get in a fight I couldn't win. I know what I need to do to win." He pulled out some notes from his pocket, looking at them for a moment. "Where is Mr. Turner?"

The crowd looked up in surprise, then a few pointed to Rafe's father, parting the way so the colonel could see him clearly.

"Ah, Mr. Turner. From the initial report I have, you carried five or six of your fellows over the silver entrance to the compound so they could escape the gunfire from inside, right?"

Rafe's father looked up in confusion.

"No, that was Rafe Turner," burst out Maria, pointing to Rafe.

"OK," the colonel replied nonplussed. "That's what I'm here for, to get the facts. So, Mr. Other Turner, was what you did good?"

Rafe felt all eyes on him. Actually, he felt pretty proud of what he had done. He had been waiting, in vain so far, to be sure, for Trevor to acknowledge that and thank him. But he certainly didn't like the attention.

"Well, yes, I guess. I mean, we got everyone out."

"Everyone?"

Rafe looked down, not wanting to catch the man's eyes. "Well, not everyone."

"And your job in this little escapade was as a driver, right?"

"Yes."

"So why didn't you get in your van, or better yet, that huge motor home you had, and drive into the compound. You could have gotten everyone in on one trip and had everyone subject to fire for a far less amount of time."

Rafe was stunned. He had never thought of that. The fact that no one else had thought of it either was no solace. But the guy was right.

"I ..., I...," he stammered out. "I never thought of that."

"Give the man a prize," the colonel said sarcastically. "You're right. You never thought. None of you thought. So now I am here to do the thinking for you."

"But we know better now. We know what we have to do," put in Trevor, seemingly not willing to give up the argument.

The colonel swung around to look at him. "And you think they're going to do the same thing? Let me tell you, young man, that this homicidal group of misfits was just as amateur as you. They sucked at their plan, too. If I had been running their ambush, none of you would have gotten out alive. But they were just as bad and incompetent as you. The problem is that they too have brains. And they're going to figure out how to do it better next time, if there is a next time, that is."

He stopped again to look at everyone. There was a nervous shuffling of feet, but no one said anything.

"OK. Sean, I need a place to work. In 15 minutes, I want to see three people who were on the rescue attempt, including that one," he said, pointing to Trevor. "He's got the fight in him, at least. Then have the tribal council stand by. I'm going to want to see them next. I've got someone else coming in tomorrow, too, so you're going to have to get someone to pick him up at the airport."

With that, and followed by Mr. Peterson, he walked out, not acknowledging anyone else. No one said a word until he left, then a cacophony of noise broke out.

"Just who the fuck does that little midget think he is? He can take me when I'm in wolf mode? I'm calling bullshit on that one!" Trevor asked no one in particular.

Rafe was already standing by him, but Erica, Tank, and a few others came to gather around.

"Really, you don't know?" asked Erica.

"Should I?"

"Well, yes, I would think you would've heard of him. That's Colonel Joshua Hartigan."

"Yeah, I already heard his name. And colonel of what? Fried chicken?"

"He was a colonel in the Marines. Kind of a hero there, I think," she replied.

"What, with jellos? So what? That makes him special how?"

"Oh, I don't know about that. But the important thing is that he's used by the Council," her emphasis on the word "council" making it clear she meant the United Tribe Council, not a local tribal council, "when there is a problem."

"Like what?"

"Like Slovakia?" asked Tank.

"Slovenia, but yes. The rouge pack of werewolves. The colonel was the guy they sent to clean it up."

"So he killed other werewolves?" Trevor asked in slight shock.

"Evidently."

"No wonder he joined a jello army. He's against us." He now looked disgusted. "How could his tribe let him do that?"

"Well, if he had a tribe, I guess 'cause it had to be done," she replied.

"What, no tribe? But that's..."

"Against the UT Charter, yes. No one is without a tribe. But he is. He's a 'member-at-large' or some such. So before you challenge him to some I-can-piss-higher-than-you contest, take a moment to think about his place in the scheme of things. Maybe you need to scale it back a notch."

Chet Craig came back in the door, spotted Trevor, and urgently motioned for him to follow.

"They want you now, so promise me you'll hold back your temper, OK?"

Trevor shrugged. "OK, for now, at least. But I'm withholding judgment until later."

Erica gave him a peck on the cheek as he pulled away to join the anxiously awaiting Chet.

"Think he'll do it?" Tank asked.

"I don't know, Tank, I don't know. I hope so."

Rafe hoped so as well. He had no love lost for Trevor, but something told him that if he tangled with their guest member-at-large, he would be coming out on the losing side of things.

Chapter 30
The next morning

Rafe walked into a community center abuzz with activity. Ignored, as usual, he kept to the outskirts of each group, listening in to see what was going on. The center of gravity was Colonel Hartigan, as could be expected. His mother was in deep conversation with the man. Another man, a stranger to Rafe, stood by. Tall and rangy, his ebony black skin seemed to hide his features. While his skin was quite dark, his features were sharper, almost Arabic-looking. Rafe wondered who he was.

As he was watching, Chet, who seemed to have inherited the gofer role, rushed up with a stack of papers.

"I got these printed out, Josh. You got any more you need?"

"No, but watch the e-mail. I'm expecting some more files."

"Roger wilco!" he almost shouted out as he wheeled about.

Roger wilco? Rafe questioned himself. *Does he realize what a dork that makes him sound like?*

The colonel handed the papers to the black man. "OK, Njaka, do your magic with these. I want a full brief on what we've got as soon as you can."

"You've got it," the man said with a heavy accent Rafe took to be African. He took the printouts and moved to a free spot on one of the many tables which had been set up.

Rafe unobtrusively wandered over to take a look. The printouts seemed to be blueprints, and as the man started to lay them out in some sort of order, Rafe suddenly recognized them as representing the God's Judgment compound.

The man, Njaka the colonel called him, started taping the individual sheets together to make one giant blueprint. One sheet fell to the floor, and Rafe stepped up to retrieve it, handing it to Njaka. The man merely grunted and took it back, his concentration centered on his work.

For the next several hours, Rafe wandered about, listening in, but never a part of any of the small groups doing their various tasks, but he kept gravitating to Njaka and his blueprints. Scribbled notes soon filled in the empty spaces between the buildings.

He was watching the man work, trying to read the scribbles, when there was a commotion at the front door. He looked up to see Alysha striding in, still naked and obviously just shifted. She was handed one of the communal robes which were kept by the main door, and as she started to say something, she was hurriedly ushered up to the colonel. Rafe joined the general mass rush to see what was going on. He didn't push his way to the front, but he could see over most of the others as Alysha was introduced to the colonel and as the colonel started questioning her.

Rafe was relieved to see her. He had played with her when they were kids together, and while they hadn't had much contact since Revelations, neither had she seemed to hold him in the same disdain as some of the others.

He wasn't close enough to catch everything, but he caught the gist of it: Alysha has seen the disaster unfolding, then had stayed to spy on what would happen after the ambush. She had watched them come out of their walls to celebrate their victory, she had watched them burn the bodies of their tribemates and her husband. The next day, she had watched them start to do some sort of work on the gateway into the compound. Eventually, her strength began to flag, and she knew she should report back, so she had started the long flight back to the tribe. Obviously exhausted, she still burned with righteous anger.

As her report ended and the ensuing questions from the colonel were answered, several members came up to give her their condolences and to let her know they were happy for her return. She didn't seem to acknowledge much of that.

Rafe wanted to go up to her himself, but he never made the move. Instead, he went into the meeting room which had been set up as a cafeteria of sorts with sandwiches, macaroni salad, and drinks offered to whoever wanted them. Taking a roast beef on a kaiser roll and a Dr. Pepper, he sat on the floor in the corner to eat. The roast beef was dry, but he didn't feel like getting up to grab some condiments, so he slowly chewed on it between swigs of his drink.

He was somewhat lost in his thoughts when Chet came up to him.

"Rafe, Colonel Hartigan wants to see you." He stood there, obviously waiting for Rafe to follow him.

The colonel wants me? he wondered. *Why me?*

He took a last swig of Dr. Pepper, then stood up, wiping his hands on his jeans. Following Chet, he went back into the main recreation room and over to the colonel. Just before reaching the busy man, Trevor intercepted him.

"You need to go on a road trip," he told him as he handed Rafe an e-ticket printout. "You're going with Shelly to Wichita to interview an electrician. Well, let me rephrase that. Shelly's doing the interview. You're just going to drive the rental car and do anything she needs."

Rafe looked down at the printout. He saw he had a flight in just under three hours from then. "Uh, why me?"

"I chose you. The colonel doesn't want anyone to go alone, and while Shelly has a way of getting things out of guys, everyone else is needed here. You're expendable, and you've got a driver's license, so you're going." He waited for some sort of reaction.

Rafe knew he should say something. He resented Trevor's smug silence. But he didn't have the energy. He just shrugged his acceptance, turned around, and went to change clothes before leaving.

Chapter 31
that evening, Wichita, Kansas

Rafe pulled up the curb. Together with Shelly, they peered through the darkness.

"14665. Yep. This is the place," Shelly announced.

They hadn't said much on the way to the airport to catch their flight. Having last-minute tickets, they hadn't even sat together on the flight itself. Rafe had gotten the rental car, and on the way to their destination, Shelly had let him know, in no uncertain terms, that she was in charge and for Rafe to just follow her lead. That was fine with him.

They walked up to the front door of the large single-floor home, and Shelly rang the doorbell. She unbuttoned another button on her blouse while waiting for the door to open. They heard footsteps, then the door opened to reveal a florid-faced man, somewhat overweight, but friendly-enough looking.

"Mr. Tremont? I'm Shelly Angeles. I believe you have been expecting us?"

Mr. Tremont held out his hand. "Please, call me Ralph. And yes, I got your people's call, and I've already got my files. Come in, come in."

He moved to the side and the two of them entered. The house was more tastefully furnished than Rafe would have guessed. The furniture was in mostly muted pastels of various colors but which seemed to mesh well together. Some modern art adorned the walls. Over the fireplace, though, was a portrait of a pleasant looking middle-aged woman holding a small dog of some sort.

Mr. Tremont, that is Ralph, caught Rafe's eyes. "That's my wife, Angela with Napoleon. I lost her two years ago in a car accident not two blocks from here. Lost Napoleon in the same accident. So now it's just me," he said with a shrug of his shoulders.

"I'm so sorry for your loss, Ralph." Shelly moved over to touch his arm as she said it.

"Ah, what's done is done." He shook his head as if resetting. "Can I get you anything to drink?"

"Oh, that's sweet of you. Coffee would be great."

"And you?" he asked Rafe.

Rafe held out his hand. "I'm Rafe Turner, by-the-way, and I'm sorry for your loss. And yes, coffee would be fine."

Shelly being in charge or not, he felt she should have introduced him. But he didn't say anything as Ralph invited them to take a seat on the couch while he went to get their coffee.

He refrained from walking around and looking at things. The house looked very nice, like a real home. Rafe wondered if MJ and he would ever have something like this together. It was too bad that Ralph had to live there alone.

Ralph came back with the coffee, which was surprisingly good. It wasn't instant, that was for sure.

"Now, your people already told me kinda what you want. I pulled all my files for God's Judgment, so I hope I can help you. What exactly do you want to know?"

"Well, Ralph," Shelly started to reply, her voice dropping a bit as she voiced his name, "we know that the church has had work done after the initial build, and that you did most of it. We don't have the records of that from the county, so we're trying to find out just what was done."

"No, you wouldn't have anything with the county records. Those people paid me extra to keep most of it off the books. How did you know I even did the work, anyway? There weren't no permits pulled."

"Well, Ralph," Shelly said in an almost conspiratorial tone as she leaned over to put her hand on his arm, "you are an honest man, and you filed the correct tax returns. So we know the work was done, just not what it was."

Ralph laughed. "What are you, the CIA?" he asked jokingly. "Ah, whatever, I don't care who you are. I never liked them no how, but you know, work's work, so I took the job. And if you want to know what work I done, well, I figure I can help you out."

"Can you give us a brief overview first? Then if we have questions, we can ask those later."

"Sure can." He grabbed his files and shuffled them around. He pulled out a rolled-up paper and opened it up. "See this one? Well, this here's the biggest job."

Rafe looked over on the coffee table on which Ralph and laid the paper. In the middle was a drawing of the compound, but surrounding it were markings on the property around it.

"Know what this is?" Ralph asked. When both shook their heads, he went on, "Well this here's a remote sensor field, like the Army has. Each of these circles," he indicated the small circles drawn around the compound, "is a sensor. If anything over 10 pounds steps near it, it sends off an alarm back in the control room. There's no way anyone can sneak up on them."

Rafe felt his heart drop. No wonder they had been ready for them when they launched their rescue attempt.

"Why would they do that? Who's going to invade them like that?" Shelly asked, more for cover than as a real question, Rafe was sure.

"The gays. They think the gays are going to march on them." He watched for their reactions. "Yeah, I know. They're pretty crazy. Gays going to go on the warpath? Well, that Jewish guy did attack one of their protests in Topeka. The cops put that guy in jail, can you believe that? But after what they said about the Jews, well, hell, I would've done the same thing, too, you know, if I was Jewish."

"So this is an anti-gay measure?"

"Well, I don't know about that. But that is what they told me. Personally, I believe in live-and-let-live, and I don't like them protesting the dead soldiers. They don't like gays, and they don't like Jews. And they don't like the Pope none, neither. So with all the crap they pull, pardon the language miss, maybe someone will come to kick their ass someday."

"So if you don't like them, why do the job?" Rafe had to ask. Shelly shot a glare at him.

Jonathan P. Brazee

"Well son, work's work. And well, my Angela, God rest her soul, well, she was at fault in the accident, and she hurt a guy. He can't do no work now, and I'm paying him what I can when I can. So I'm in no position to turn down good-paying work."

"No one is accusing you of anything, Ralph. But I have to ask, where did you get the sensors? They are hardly something you can pick up at Home Depot."

"Army surplus. These are old models, Vietnam era. I got them at a government auction, can you believe that? I've had them for quite awhile with no use for them, but then Jack--that's Jack Kipper—hooked me up with them."

"Well, and I know you understand that this is a delicate question, how would someone, well, ..."

"How would you get through the sensors with tripping them?"

"Well, yes, to be blunt."

Ralph laughed. "No problem with me, miss. As I told you, I don't like these folks. They're un-American, if you ask me. If someone, not you, of course, but if someone wanted to break into the compound, well they would have to turn off the sensor field. Of course, how you get in to do that, well, I don't have no answer for that."

"And, say, if someone did get in unnoticed, how would they turn off the sensors?"

"Oh, that's easy." He rummaged around his papers and pulled out a photo of what looked like a control room. "Here's my finished job photo. You see up here?" he asked pointing to a large blue switch about 5 feet off the ground. "All you have to do is pull that switch. Poof, no sensors."

"And the red switch?" Shelly asked, pointing to the equally large red switch to its left.

"Hmm, that's the, I think that's the front gate switch. Let me check." He pulled out a diagram and studied it for a moment. "Yep, that one controls the power to the front gate. The control to actually open and shut it is over on this panel," he told them, pointing to another part of the drawing. "And there's another one at the gate itself. Then this big one over here is the main power breaker. And then this one ..."

"Ralph," Shelly started, voice oozing honey, "would it be possible for us to get a copy of this?"

Ralph chuckled and replied, "I figured you'd be asking, so I already got you a copy of everything." He handed Shelly a folder full of papers.

Shelly actually squeaked as she took the folder, then moved over to give Ralph a hug around his neck. "You're a doll, Ralph!"

"My pleasure, miss. I don't want to know who you are or what you've got planned, but anything you've got planned will be well-deserved, if you ask me. And if I can do anything more to help, just call me."

"Ralph, if we can reward you in any way, I'm sure I can get our bosses to authorize ..."

He cut her off with a raised hand. "Don't you worry about me. I don't need much, and Steve Kramer, the man Angela hurt, well, I'm good with him. So you just take that and do what you have to do."

They sat around for another 20 minutes while Ralph went over other aspects of the work he had done on the compound, but Rafe could see the death-grip Shelly had on the folder. So sooner than they had to in order to catch the flight back, they made their goodbyes and got back into the car.

Shelly waved at Ralph as they pulled out and started down the road.

"Don't you think you were laying it on a bit strong?" Rafe asked her as they settled in for the drive back to the airport.

"What do you mean?" she asked.

"All the flirting, the simpering?"

"Hey, we got what we wanted." Shelly's "sweet-girl" persona had already vanished to be replaced by a hard, calculating woman.

"I just think it was inappropriate. He was obviously anxious to help us. And his wife had just died not too long ago. I think you went overboard."

"Oh, eat me," she retorted with a sneer on her face before shifting her body away from him to stare out the window.

Nothing else was said between them all the way back to the tribe.

Chapter 32
the next morning

Rafe had slept later than normal after taking the late flight back, then having to listen to Shelly brief the colonel and his team. Even getting up late, he still hadn't much sleep. He walked into the community center still rubbing his eyes.

There seemed to be a heightened sense of purpose and determination amongst both those actually working and those merely sitting and observing. There were probably too many people in the center, but Rafe figured that the colonel knew people had to be there, so he let them be.

Jaira was with the others there, so there had been no breakfast at his house when he woke up. He wandered over the meeting room, poured himself a styrofoam cup of coffee, and rummaged in the mostly empty boxes until he found a glazed doughnut. Munching on that, he wandered back into the main room to see if he could find out what was happening.

He pulled up a seat next to Jaira. "So what's going on?"

Jaira had been civil with him since his First Shift, and even friendly to an extent. As a jackal herself, maybe not being the most powerful were was something she understood.

"Colonel Josh, he told us we are going through with a rescue. Your mom, she was really happy for that, I can tell you. We're going tonight. I guess there's some things he has to fix, some problems. But he got those vultures from Ft. Collins—I forgot their names—in the air now, looking at that place. And from what they say, Colonel Josh thinks we have to go now or maybe we can't do anything."

"Thanks. Do you know who is on the rescue team?" he asked, offering Jaira a sip of his coffee.

She waved the coffee away. "Don't know. Not me, for sure. But some, you can already tell."

She motioned at a group of the more, well, alpha types, sitting in a group to the side of the colonel's planning cell, not doing anything, but still obviously part of the plan.

Trevor was still part of the colonel's cadre, but he kept going to that other group to talk/brief/whatever to them. His position of authority seemed to be growing every hour. Rafe hated that, but if it got Tabitha back any sooner, he would get on his belly and lick Trevor's feet.

Rafe watched for awhile, catching snippets of conversation around him, but not really being part of any serious discourse. He finally noticed that the coffee in his cup was cold, so he got up to refill it.

Some of the younger kids, pre-First Shift, were busy setting out sandwiches for lunch, but no one else was there as he filled his cup with fresh coffee. He turned around and almost ran over the colonel. He stepped back.

"Excuse me!" he said as he danced to keep from spilling his coffee on the smaller man.

"So you're a rat?" the colonel asked him without preamble.

Rafe felt his face get red. *Why is he asking me this?* he wondered.

"Are you?"

"Uh, yes."

"Shift." He pulled a medallion out of his pocket and threw it on the floor at Rafe's feet.

"What?"

"I think that is pretty clear. You are a wererat. I want to see you shift. So do it."

"But, I . . ." he stammered, looking around at the people gathering to see what was going on.

"Look, you either are a wererat or not. Simple. And I want you to shift. Now." The colonel looked up at him with steely eyes.

Rafe hadn't shifted since Claire was murdered, and that was an involuntary shift. He had vowed never to shift again. Oh, on occasion, he had felt the urge, but he had beaten that back. Now, when his rat ever did make its presence known, it was to poke his nose out of a hole somewhere deep within his psyche, only to scurry back into the darkness.

And now this dictator, this demigod has the balls to come in here and tell him to shift? To let the rat out again? And in front of the tribe, people who had never seen him in his rat form? Panic began to fill his senses.

The colonel reached up and grabbed his shirt. "Look, Turner," he said evenly, but with force. "I need to see you shift. And you are going to shift or I am going to pull your animal form out of your throat if I have to. Have I made myself clear?"

Rafe's will crumbled under the onslaught of the colonel's will. He nodded, and with tears welling in his eyes, he slowly took off his clothes until he stood naked before the colonel. More people crowded the doorway to watch his humiliation.

"Well?" the colonel asked impatiently.

Rafe ignored the medallion and reached within himself. He hadn't done this for a long time, and he felt rusty, if that was the right word for it. Once again, while he knew the rat was him and he was the rat, it helped him a bit to think of the rat as another creature which had to be coaxed out. He called to it. And there was a stirring, but a stirring of something afraid, something which wanted to stay in the dark, out-of-sight.

He reached out for it again. He could imagine it poking its nose out of a hole, seeing if it was safe. Willing it out, he forgot his vow, his efforts to suppress the rat within him. He felt a sudden flow of power, of "rightness." This is who he was supposed to be. A were. And suddenly he was.

He hadn't shifted in a long, long time, but he felt natural as a rat. It was as he had been bound for years, and only now were those bindings removed. He looked up with his blurry vision to see the colonel looming over him. He stared defiantly back.

The colonel suddenly reached out and snatched Rafe, picking him up by the tail. Rafe had to resist sinking his teeth into the man's hand. He brought Rafe up almost to eye level, then hefted him up and down, as if weighing him. The huge head paused, then nodded. He bent over to place Rafe back on the ground, then turned and walked away.

Rafe was more aware of the others watching him than actually seeing them. His rat vision worked better on moving objects than still, and most of the people were motionless as they watched him. Part of him wanted to slink away, to find someplace where he could be alone and drink back in the senses he had been denying himself for so many years. But he was still acutely aware of the others. So with a human-like sigh, he shifted back.

Slowly getting dressed, he ignored the others. He heard a few sniggers, a few comments at his expense thought to be funny. But he acted as he hadn't heard anything. Tightening up his belt, he ran his hand through his hair, then walked out of the meeting room. Those there parted like the Red Sea before him as he left the building and went back home.

Chapter 33
later that afternoon

Rafe decided that he couldn't hide himself away. He was what he was. The main thing now was to get Tabitha back, and he wanted to see how that was going to happen.

He walked back to the community center, steeled himself, and walked in—to an almost deserted building. Wondering where everyone was, he noticed a large paper posted on the board with the words "Rescue Team" written on the top.

He went over to read it, and as he expected, it was a list of those weres assigned to the mission. And also as he expected, his name wasn't on the list. His mom's name was there, though, as part of the assault force. Rafe figured she would be on the other force, the rescue force, which surely was the force which would rescue the two girls.

There were more people assigned to this rescue than on the first one. This would take up a good chunk of the tribe's adult population. Looking over the list, it seemed to comprise most of the more ferocious, as it were, of the weres. The strongest and most dangerous. The colonel and the African guy were there, of course, as well. One startling omission was his dad. He wasn't on any of the teams.

The rescue was broken down into five teams: assault, rescue, recon, headquarters, and support. Recon consisted of Alysha, Tank, and a few other names that Rafe did not recognize, probably raptors from other tribes. Jaira had mentioned vultures from Ft. Collins that morning.

Support consisted of primarily smaller weres. Jaira had been wrong in that she was not going to be involved; she was listed as part of that team.

The rescue team had Shelly, Jerome Sykes (Greg's brother), Kristen McConnell (a rather young wolf), Ron Amos, and to Rafe's surprise, Mr. Peterson. Surely he had to be too old to be included?

The colonel, the African, and old Mrs. Savior were in the headquarters, and the rest were in the assault team. Mrs. Savior was a cheetah, so maybe she was a messenger?

A youngster walked out of the meeting room carrying a full trash can.

"Hey, where's everyone?" Rafe asked him.

"Out past the basketball court, practicing," he was told.

Practicing? Basketball? Rafe was confused.

He walked though the center and out the back door. There, around the basketball court and in the fields on the other side, the rescue force was congregated. The colonel had a large number of people around him, and he was in full flame mode.

"You've got to get this down! We don't have time for idiots here, and you better be 100% sure that if we can't pull this together, I'm going to pull the plug on this!" he shouted out.

"But we already know what we're supposed to do," came a voice from the crowd.

"Do you think anything goes according to plan? And what are you going to do when you're hit with a nasty surprise? Growl and show your fangs? These bastards aren't likely to be cowed just because a big bad werewolf howls at them."

He paused for a moment before calling out, "You there! Mike, isn't it? What is the 'danger-attack' call for a wolf?"

"I don't know. I'm a bear. How do I know what a wolf says?"

"So you're going into battle, and make no mistake, this will be a battle, and you don't know how to communicate with each other? That's going to get you killed!"

"But you gave us these radio things," Trevor responded, pointing to a small object that looked velcroed to each person's arm. Rafe hadn't noticed them before.

"And if I'm taken out? If you are all in animal form? You still cannot communicate with each other. So let's go through this again, from the beginning. Now!"

Rafe noticed markers on the ground in the field. They roughly replicated the God's Judgment compound. The teams slowly congregated back inside the basketball court, then at the colonel's signal, they moved out, growling and yelling, but still in human form. And the colonel ran alongside of them, yelling, berating, instructing, and physically pulling and pushing people into position as they moved at 3/4 speed into the mock attack.

Once, when he yanked Trevor to point him in a new direction, Trevor snapped.

"Who the fuck do you think you are? What makes you the supposed expert?" he exploded, saliva spewing from his mouth.

The colonel merely looked at him, then said, "I've been in combat. I have watched my men die. And I have watched them defeat the enemy. Have you?"

"Yeah, you've watched jellos die, good riddance," Trevor retorted.

There was a flurry of motion, and Trevor was on the ground, the colonel standing over him. Rafe thought he could see the colonel waver as if he had started to shift, then stop himself.

"Those were my men, human beings, just like you. Some could do things you could never dream of doing. And they were much better fighters than you will ever hope to be! And if you ever put them down again, I swear I will tear out your throat!"

The venom could almost be felt as everyone stopped and watched in shock.

Trevor wasn't done yet. Cowed a bit, but not done.

He looked up and said in a calmer, more dismissing voice, "Yeah, the big hero. Fighting your jello wars. What would they say if they knew you were a were-whatever-the-hell-you-are? That a bullet wasn't going to kill you like it would them? That you had 'powers?' You put them in danger when you weren't in the same situation. You weren't in danger yourself."

There was a collective gasp as people waited for the colonel to explode. But he stepped back, looked to the sky, and told him, "That is something that has bothered me every day of my life. I sent men to die, knowing that I wasn't sharing their same peril. I will take that with me to the grave."

He turned around, looking at all the silent people. "Who told you to stop? No matter what happens, you've got to keep moving! Let's go!"

Rafe sat down with his back against a tree as he watched the rescue force go through their paces again and again. He thought it was kind of silly to be doing it so many times in human form, but he guessed it did make it easier to communicate. And the pattern of the assault began to resonate with him. He could see how the components meshed. He had to admit that this made their original attempt to rescue the girls strictly amateur.

A new truck had been added to the rescue effort. It was bigger than a pick-up, but not like a semi. Frankly, Rafe hadn't seen one like this. This truck seemed to be the lead vehicle in the assault. The driver was a young man who clearly relished his task. He drove through the "gate" of the compound, slamming to a stop as the assault team jumped out.

"Why don't you bring in a rhino from another tribe?" asked Shelly after the truck driver ran over the tape designating the gateway walls for the second time in a row.

The colonel stopped and motioned others to come in closer.

"This is what I'm trying to teach you. You all feel that by shifting, you can do anything. But you've got to remember that sometimes, your human form is more capable. And that technology is not evil. You want a rhino? What do you think will happen if one of our rhino brothers hits a reinforced gate here? You think he's going to have more power than our truck here, if Stan here can drive it straight? We've got to use all our resources.

"Look, we are all blessed with a gift, a special gift. And that gift gives us power. But we have to know when to take from the human side of us, both in form and with our tools. Understand?" He really seemed to be trying to reach out to them.

"OK, let's take a 10-minute break. Chet, let's get out the carriers. I want everyone to get the right carrier for your animal form. I've got somebody at each station to tell you where to put it on while in human mode so that it is in place after you shift. It doesn't make sense to have a belt around your 32-inch waist before you shift into a bear with a 100 inch waist, right? After you have the right carrier, let's get outfitted up with whatever gear you've been assigned. Our next rehearsal is in full were mode, so let's get cracking."

There was loud roar of approval from the tired people, people anxious to shift into their more wild personas. Rafe shifted his weight from where he was sitting. He thought this should be pretty interesting. The rescue team had been put through their paces in human form. He wondered if everyone would forget their missions once in animal form.

Most people forgot that they were on a 10-minute break as they immediately hurried to the various stations which corresponded with their animal forms. They were anxious to forge ahead. The carriers were little more than flexible belts, connected by velcro, which had slots or sheaths for carrying items. Depending on the animal form, these were placed around arms, waists, or legs. The idea, as explained, was that when a person shifted from human to animal or back, the carrier belt would remain with that person.

This wouldn't work with the com devices, though. They had to be emplaced once a person was in animal form. A small receiver on a wolf just would not correspond to a human body and would fall off. Of course, a human could then pick it up and hold it to his or her ear to get instructions.

Jonathan P. Brazee

Most people, after being fitted with their carrier, shifted back and forth a few times, checking the viability of the concept. Many carriers had to be adjusted in order to survive the shift. It took almost an hour before everyone was ready for the first shift despite the repeated urgings of the colonel and Chet. Rafe had plenty of time to wander over to the snack table to snag a tuna sandwich and a Coke while people got ready.

He was back at his tree when the first shifted rehearsal took place. Predictably, at least to him, the rehearsal was a disaster. All the lessons of the walk-throughs seemed to have disappeared as wolves, bears, coyotes, hyenas, and other weres ran amok. One familiar tiger seemed bent on reaching the area where the girls were thought to be held rather than focusing on her assignment. Rafe winced as he watched that.

The colonel blasted his whistle over and over again to call a halt to the rehearsal. It took awhile, but everyone made it back to the starting point.

The colonel was livid, his face red as he screamed at them. He took particular issue with Rafe's mother.

"What is God's name do you think you were doing? Did you forget everything we have done so far?" he screamed in fury.

"That's my daughter there, and I need to get her!" she shouted back.

"You're a tiger, for God's sake! You are perhaps the best fighting form out there. Maybe not as strong as one of our bears, but as a killing machine, you need to be assaulting the enemy. Leave the rescue to the team selected. They will act in *unison*," he emphasized the word, "to get into the building and rescue the girls. If you get there alone, what do you think will happen? How are you going to get inside, and more importantly, while you're out there growling, do you think any guard is going to let the girls live? Really?"

"I ... but I want to ..."

"You want to get your daughter killed? Then by all means charge away like the Lone Ranger. But I am telling you now, I will pull you from this mission if you can't follow orders. Understand?"

Rafe doubted if he had ever seen his mother glare at anyone like that. He expected the colonel to wither under that glare, but the man never faltered. After a few tense moments, his mother backed down.

"OK, no need for that. I'll do as you say, but so help me, that rescue team better get my daughter out."

The colonel nodded, before addressing the rest. "OK, let's do it again. At half speed, if you please. Remember everything we went over before and remember your assigned task!"

Once again, it took longer than what Rafe felt was necessary to get going, but soon enough, the entire rescue effort was walking through their paces at half-speed. And it was going much better.

Half-way through the walkthrough, Rafe saw Njaka return from somewhere and go up to the colonel. Rafe was pretty far away, but it looked as if he was indicating something negative to the colonel. The colonel listened intently and asked something back, to which Njaka shook his head. The colonel slammed his whistle into the ground, then stood for a moment, hands on his hips. He seemed to shrug his shoulders, then looked up, searching the staging area for the rehearsals. It took a moment, but his eyes found and locked onto Rafe's. With his right hand up and forefinger extended, he motioned for Rafe to come to him.

Oh shit, he thought. *What now?*

But he dutifully stood up and made the long walk to where the colonel and Njaka were standing. He approached them feeling apprehensive inside, but he kept his head high and his outer appearance confident (he hoped.)

"I'm putting you in the game," the colonel said as he walked up, hand held out to shake.

Rafe automatically took the hand, but he was surprised.

"What, as a driver?" He wished he could do more, but if he could contribute in anyway, then a driver was fine.

"No, I need you for a special mission. You're going to take Njaka's place for this."

Rafe looked over at the African who merely shrugged apologetically.

"But . . . he's part of your team. I mean, what can I do that he can't?"

"You can walk up to the compound," was the simple reply.

"I don't understand."

"Njaka is my right-hand man. Not only is he great with building plans, electrical plans, all those plans, but he is an infiltrator extraordinaire. He can get into almost anywhere." He reached over to clap Njaka on the shoulder while he said this.

"So what has that got to do with me?" the confused Rafe asked.

"One reason that Njaka excels at what he does is that he's a fossa." He held up his hand to stop Rafe's obvious question. "A fossa is a tree-climbing predator native to Madagascar. If you saw the cartoon movie *Madagascar*, well, the bad guys were the fossa."

"Bad rap," muttered Njaka.

The colonel rolled his eyes as the comment. "The problem is that Njaka comes in at about 20 pounds in his animal form. That's really small for a were, but . . ." he told Rafe, waiting for him to see the point.

Rafe stared at the man for a moment before comprehension lit his eyes. "The sensors! They take 10 pounds to set off. So when you told us that the sensors would be turned off before our assault, you planned on Njaka to do that!"

"Right. So we need someone who is smaller than that, someone who can sneak around unobserved to turn off the sensors."

More comprehension dawned on Rafe. "And that's why you picked me up, to see what I weighed."

"Right again. To be honest, I was hoping that Njaka would still be able to take the mission, but after testing himself all day, he can't. And that's why I held you out of any team assignment. I figured you might have to be used, so I didn't want to disrupt any other team." He looked closely into Rafe's eyes. "So are you up for it?"

"Yes, sir! Just tell me what to do."

"I'm going to turn you over to Njaka for that. I've got to get this cluster unscrewed if the mission will proceed at all." He turned back to the African. "Njaka, he's all yours."

They both watched the colonel suddenly run off as he spotted something which needed his immediate and forceful attention.

"You ready there, son?" Njaka asked him.

"You bet."

"Then come with me."

Njaka turned to walk back towards the community center. Rafe felt 10 feet tall as he followed, heart pounding with excitement.

Chapter 34
later that night

The colonel had decided that the team was not ready, so he postponed the operation by a day, warning everyone that if they weren't ready after one more day, he was pulling the plug on the entire operation. After some cross words with Rafe's mother and Katie's father after that pronouncement, he sent everyone home to get some much-needed rest.

Rafe, however, was still in one of the offices with Njaka, going over the plan. Rafe knew Njaka was a seasoned professional with a number of missions for the United Tribes under his belt, and he knew he needed to cram the same capabilities within a very short period of time. The one-day delay helped, but Rafe didn't hold out much hope that he would be completely up to speed by the time the rescue attempt kicked off.

Basically, the plan seemed straightforward. Rafe, in rat form, would ride Jeremy Parkinson, in wolf form, to the north side of the compound, 50 yards or so outside of the sensored area. From there, he would make his way over the sensor field and to the compound walls. Wearing leather booties and with his claws painted with a shellac, he would climb the outside walls to the roof, then down an air vent which led to the control room.

Inside the control room, he had two tasks. One was to shut off the sensor field. The other was to disable the front gate. Reports from the eyes on target indicated that work was being done to the door, making it sturdier. So the colonel wanted it disabled.

As a rat, he couldn't really flip the switches, so he would have to shift back to human form before doing that. But the fact that he would be in a control room where certainly there would be someone on duty put a "wrinkle" on things, as Njaka referred to it. To Rafe, it was more of a barrier.

In an attempt to get past that barrier, Njaka was trying to teach Rafe the basics of knife combat. Rafe was not doing too well.

Njaka reached out and slapped Rafe hard on the face.

"Keep your free hand up!"

Rafe raised his left hand up a bit, but Njaka quickly slapped his face again, going around Rafe's upraised hand.

Rafe stepped back in exasperation.

"I just can't get it!" he complained.

Njaka looked at him for a moment, them motioned him to take a seat. Rafe pulled one of the office chairs from the corner where it had been shoved and sat down wearily. He looked at his watch. They had been going over this for more than an hour.

"I know this is difficult. But if there is someone there, you have to be able to neutralize him."

"You mean kill him."

"Neutralize him. Kill him, yes, that is one way." Njaka's heavy accent somehow seemed to lessen the impact of them speaking about killing another human being. "But putting him down and out of action is also OK. Or if he does not interfere with you, doing nothing is OK. All you have to do is throw the two switches. You have to do that, and before the assault team hits that gate. Everything else is secondary." He paused again. "So that's why you have to know how to use a knife. That may be all you can carry in with you. I can bring a gun as a fossa, but that's going to be too big for you. So let's get up and try again."

Rafe sighed and stood. Pushing the chair back, he held the pencil which was taking the place of a knife in the underhand position Njaka had been drilling into him. And for the next 30 minutes, he feinted, parried, and thrust at Njaka's instructions. At one point, the colonel stuck his head in and looked at the African with raised eyebrows in an obvious question. Rafe caught the slight shake of Njaka's head before the colonel left.

Jonathan P. Brazee

"OK, let's stop. We'll go over more tomorrow morning.
One thing to remember, though, is if you hesitate, you are
going to lose. You've got to be in attack mode. This guy, or
girl, for that matter, is going to be shocked when a 6'2" naked
man suddenly materializes in that room. There's going to be
panic. So take advantage of that. Rush him! Don't give him
time to think. That's 3/4 of the battle right there.   Of any
battle. *Capice?*"

Rafe smiled at hearing Italian with a heavy African
accent. *"Capice,"* he replied.

"OK, then. Why don't you go home and get some sleep.
I want to see you back here at . . ." he looked at his watch. ". . .
at 8:00, OK?"

"Sure."

Rafe got up and started to walk out.

"Rafe!"

Rafe turned around and looked back.

"You're going to do fine."

I sure hope so, the thought, as he walked out the center
and into the night.

Chapter 35
7:50 AM the next morning

Rafe hurried into the community center. Despite getting home quite late, he hadn't slept much. His mind had churned with emotions vacillating between excitement, pride that he could contribute, and worry about Tabitha. Finally, the clock edged closer and closer to 8:00, and he was able to get back to the center.

Jaira's housekeeping duties had changed for the duration, so there had been nothing to eat. Rafe was pretty hungry, so he went to get coffee and doughnuts. Taking three of them (a glazed, a jelly, and a chocolate-covered cake doughnut) he moved to the side to let others help themselves. He spotted Alysha sitting alone in the corner, and after a bit of gathering up himself, he walked over to her.

Rafe had never been particularly close to Alysha, even before First Shift. They had been friendly, but not friends. She had been a somewhat strange girl, seeing the world through different eyes. Maybe that was the raptor in her, but more likely, that was just her human side. Some people just seemed to march to a different drummer. But still, she was part of his year group, and she had suffered a loss. And suffering a loss was something Rafe understood.

She didn't look up as he stood over her.

"Alysha, I just wanted to say—"

"Can it," she interrupted him, still not looking up.

Rafe hunched back a bit in confusion, then tried again, "I just wanted to tell you that I'm—"

"What part of 'can it' don't you understand, rat-boy?" Now she looked up, anger blazing from her eyes.

"But—"

She stood up and put a finger in his chest. "Get away from me. I don't need your sympathy. Got it? All this is pretty much your fault. Yours and the rest of this pathetic tribe. If you were anything other than a freaking rat, maybe you could have stopped this back then before things escalated. And if General-of-the-Frigging-Army Trevor had an ounce of brains, then that fiasco would never have happened. And you had to drag my Tom into it, didn't you. And Tom, it wasn't his fight, you know, but he just had to volunteer to help. And now he's gone. And for what? For your sister? For Katie?" She paused for a moment, chest heaving, tears welling in her eyes. "Let me be perfectly clear. I'm here only to relish the destruction of that abomination that calls itself a church. And once they are all rotting in hell, all of you can join them there for all I care. I'll be done with you all. Take that to the bank, Mr. Rat!"

She turned and strode off as Rafe stood there in shock before half-collapsing into the chair in which she had been sitting. He hadn't been prepared for that onslaught. And he felt guilty. His excitement of being able to contribute faded as his psyche grabbed the guilt he had tried to hide and dragged it to the surface. Alysha was right. He was useless as a were. If he had been anything else, if he had had any other animal form, then maybe Claire would still be alive.

"Hey, you ready to hit it?" Njaka's voice interrupted his pity party.

He stood there with a backpack in hand, waiting for a response.

Rafe wondered if he was really up to it, but he merely nodded and stood back up, then followed him out of the building and around in back. Njaka reached in his backpack and took out what looked to be four small leather pouches. Despite himself, Rafe looked on with interest.

"It took some effort, but we made these gloves for you. We need to test them first, though. We'll shellac your nails before the actual operation, but for now, we got to see if you can climb stucco with these on."

"Gloves?"

"You going to climb silver treated walls with your bare paws?" Njaka asked him, his face twisted in a grimace.

Rafe had forgotten that part of the plan. Of course he needed protection, and Njaka had mentioned the gloves the day before.

Stopping before the back wall of the recreation center, Njaka said, "And here's our wall. Only one story, true, but we should be able to test to see if these work OK. So go ahead and shift and let's get going."

Rafe quickly disrobed. His interest was up, and he shifted to his rat before he realized it. Njaka picked him up to his shoulder, then took each leather pouch and slid them over Rafe's paws, front and back. Rafe felt quite weird being handled, to be truthful. He didn't like it. His instincts screamed at him to run, but he was able to keep that in check.

The little gloves had holes in them so his claws could protrude, but the leather felt confining. He didn't know if they would hamper him too much.

Njaka placed him on the ground at the base of the back wall. "OK, Rafe, up you go."

Rafe looked up. As usual in his rat mode, his eyesight was not that great, and the somewhat blurry wall rose above him seemingly up to the sky. He moved forward a bit, getting the feel of the gloves. Right at the wall, he reached up and tentatively touched it with one paw.

"Don't massage it, climb!" Njaka's voice boomed out, filling the air much more than when listened to it with human ears.

Well, there was nothing else to do except attack it. With a jump, Rafe grabbed the wall a good two feet up. "Grabbed" would not be the appropriate terms had he been in human form, but with his claws, he could literally grab onto the uneven surfaces of the stucco. He started to scramble up when a huge hand grabbed him by the tail and pulled him off the wall, holding him upside down in front of his looming face. Anger started to build as he looked up at Njaka.

"Your tail? Do you think it is immune to the silver? Keep it off the wall!"

Njaka placed him back down on the grass while Rafe would have hit himself in the forehead with a "Duh!" if he could have. He readied himself again, this time concentrating on touching the wall only with his paws. He jumped up and immediately lost his grip to fall back. He tried again only to fall back once more.

"Wait, let me think," Njaka boomed out again.

Rafe could barely make out the big man staring at the wall.

"I think it's your center of gravity. When you hold yourself off the wall, your center of gravity is too off-balance, and you fall over. OK, go ahead and hug the wall for now. We'll have to make you a shirt or something to keep you out of direct contact with it."

Rafe nodded, then realizing that was a pretty human gesture. Turning back around, he leapt again, this time hugging the wall. And he stayed on. He tried to start moving up, sort of pushing off with his back legs, then grabbing with his front. He made it two leaps before falling back to the ground.

"If you jump too far that way, you're going to be too far off to catch a hold, and your center of gravity is going to be too far off again. Try one leg at a time, keeping three in contact with the wall at all times."

Through trial and error, and with numerous falls, Rafe finally got the knack of it. He could make it up to the top without falling. The gloves were cumbersome, but he could still manage the climb.

Coming down was fun. With his body as light as it was, he could simply jump down. The first time he did it, he jumped on Njaka's shoulder. Njaka jumped back in startlement, then laughed. Rafe felt that even with the higher walls of the compound, he could probably jump off them if he had to.

"OK, time for the next step. Come over here and let me get this on you."

Rafe dutifully scampered over while Njaka dug in his backpack, pulling out some kind of strapping. He adjusted in it around Rafe's torso. If Rafe didn't like hands touching him, this was worse. It felt confining, restricting.

"Reach down here. Can you reach it OK?"

Rafe felt to his belly where Njaka was indicating. He nodded his answer.

"OK, this is the release. You should be able to activate it. You're going to need to release this carrier before shifting back."

Njaka continued with a few adjustments, then Rafe could hear him rustle in his backpack again. The smell of what Rafe recognized as gunpowder quickly washed over him, and Njaka placed something in his carrier. Rafe knew immediately that it was a gun.

As with all weres, Rafe was much stronger than the regular animals from which he took his animal form. For a rat, he was pretty darn strong. The weight of the handgun might burden a normal rat, but he was OK with it.

"OK, let's try and climb with that in your carrier," Njaka told him.

Rafe moved to the wall and began his ascent. *Began* was the operable word, because no matter how hard he tried, he could not seem to keep his grip, and he crashed to the ground over and over.

"I was afraid of that," Njaka told him after he called off the attempts. "You can carry the weight, but we get to the same thing with your center of gravity. Oh well, we had to try it, but I think you're going to have to rely on the knife."

A gun might have been nice to have. Rafe figured it would have given him a better chance to take out anyone in the control room. He was still not too confident with his skill as a knife-fighter.

Rafe was getting extremely hungry, so he was quite happy when Njaka called a stop to things. He quickly shifted back. With his superior human eyes, he was surprised to see that quite a few people had been observing his training. He couldn't tell from their expressions what they thought, but if anything, he imagined he saw at least some degree of disapproval. He got dressed while Njaka went over the session. Nothing Njaka said was new, and he really wanted to get in and eat. Only the last thing Njaka said really registered.

"Just remember that this rescue attempt depends on you. If you don't get your job done, we'll never get off the ground. So whatever you have to do, just do it. Obstacles don't exist, right?"

"Don't worry," Rafe responded. "I'll get it done."

"I have full confidence that you will."

Chapter 36
two miles outside the God's Judgment Compound late the next evening

Rafe looked at the rescue force resolutely getting ready. He couldn't believe they were actually doing this, but the colonel had given his go-ahead the evening before, and they had driven through the night and most of the day to get to the compound. Remembering what had happened the last time they were here, Rafe's initial excitement had been replaced a bit with anxiety. Add the pressure being put on him to kick things off, and his anxiety level was rising by the minute.

They were out-of-sight of the compound, which was hidden by a low hill and trees, and well off any road, but lights were off so as to keep any unexpected eyes from spotting them. Most of them were still in human form, but several bears were getting outfitted with the battering rams which would be used to batter open the doors going into the buildings proper. They couldn't use the rams themselves in bear form, but they were the only ones with the strength, really, to carry them. Well, that was not quite true. A werewolf could certainly carry the weight, but the shape of the rams would make a werewolf out of balance and awkward carrying one. So the werebears it was. Once in position, other weres would shift back to human form to do the actual battering.

According to the building plans, the doors themselves were metal, so no one knew if they were coated with the silver solution. While the stucco would easily retain a solution like that, it didn't seem likely that a smooth metal door could retain it. That possibility, though, had to be kept in mind when assaulting each door.

"You ready, Rafe?" Njaka, coming up in back of him, asked.

"Sure, I guess. I mean sure."

Jonathan P. Brazee

He slowly took off his clothes. Looking once again over the hill which blocked their view of the compound, he easily shifted. The far-off view disappeared to be replaced by milling shapes. One of them, he knew, was Mrs. St. John. He picked her out by smell. Rafe still thought it was odd that he could use his nose so well when the telltale clues were part of his human side of life. He guessed his subconscious always knew what Mrs. St. John smelled like, but while his human nose didn't make the connection, his rat nose did.

She took a seat on a folding chair, then motioned for him to jump in her lap. She had a plastic sheet placed there, onto which Rafe settled. Carefully, she took each of his paws in turn, using a small fingernail polish brush to apply the special shellac to each claw which supposedly would protect him from the silver. After coating the claws on each paw, she blew on them, just as she probably blew on her own nails when putting polish on them.

Finally, she was done, and she stood up to pass him back to Njaka. Once in Njaka's grasp, though, she gave his head a little pat. That was a far cry from when she tried to wipe off her hands after touching him, back after his First Shift. That probably never registered to her, but it did to Rafe.

Rafe suffered through the little shirt and the carrier being put on, the small ceramic knife going into the sheath, the earpiece for the com being attached, and the booties being tied on. He still hated the handling, but he endured it stoically.

Njaka finished prepping him, then put him on the ground and stepped back. He spoke into a small mic.

"Do you copy?" came over the small earpiece.

Copy? he wondered to himself. *Yes I "hear" you, not "copy" you.*

He couldn't say that, of course, so he merely squeaked and nodded. It was easier to do that than to reach back and press the send button, which would only give a click as it was.

Njaka stepped back. "Where's Jeremy? He needs to be here now."

Rafe could hear him both directly and over the earpiece. Njaka needed to be careful about keeping the com keyed. As long as he did that, no one else could transmit. Rafe wanted to tell him that, but he couldn't shift back and still keep all his attachments attached.

It took a few minutes, but a smallish wolf finally trotted up. Rafe had met Jeremy only on the ride up, which was appropriate as Jeremy was his ride here. Two miles was too far for a rat to move in any reasonable amount of time, but for a wolf, it was easy. A strap had been rigged around Jeremy's chest, and with one bound, Rafe jumped on his back, then held onto the strap. He felt a bit like the cowboys he had seen on television, the ones strapping their hands onto an angry bull. He hoped the analogy was misplaced.

Rafe sensed more than saw others beginning to shift. With the assault planned for a little more than two hours away, they didn't have to shift yet, but people were evidently anxious to get going.

Rafe had no trouble identifying the colonel when he walked up.

"You two ready?" he asked them, then going on before either one of them could respond, "Don't cut any corners. I want you to take the long way around, as we showed you. Tank dropped the scent pack to let you know you're there. And you," he pointed to the wolf, "under no circumstances, get any closer than that. Understand?"

Jeremy nodded his understanding.

Jonathan P. Brazee

"OK, you've both got the earpieces, and we're going to keep the channel clear as much as possible. But if anything happens to our com, Turner, you're to start moving in at 0100," he said, pronouncing the time as "zero-one-hundred." "You need to be in place by 0145, and at 0215, you've got to cut the power to both the sensors and the gate." He looked around for a moment before continuing in a lower voice. "Look, some new information has come in, and we think they've reinforced the gate. And I don't know that we can ram it, even with the truck. So if you can't get it done, well, the whole rescue might have to be scrapped. So it really is up to you. At about 0217, we're going to be charging in, and that gate's got to be open."

Rafe felt the world getting heavier. He knew if this raid didn't succeed, there probably would not be another attempt. It was do or die here.

"OK, you two get going. God speed."

Rafe wanted to respond, but before he could even think of a gesture which would have meaning, Jeremy had wheeled about and was trotting off. Rafe started bouncing up and down, but while it was uncomfortable and frankly annoying, he had no real problem staying on his back. Wolves, it seemed, didn't make the best steeds.

Rafe couldn't see well enough to make out too many details of the route to the compound, so he just took in the smells which came to him. The night was full of heavy, moist smells: of mildew, of grass, of flowers. Of water, flowing slowly in creeks. Of mice scurrying about their nightly tasks. Of a deer bounding away, his musk emitting clear panic at a wolf loping by. Of more than a few rotting corpses and the beetles feeding on them. Of urine and droppings, the signposts of life.

Rafe was amazed at it all, the rich diversity of the night. He wondered how his human self had gone through life blind to all of this.

Jeremy loped through the woods, a furry taxi. He moved effortlessly through the brush and trees. He made a huge loop to enable them to come up behind the compound. Before long, the smell of jasmine, the aroma used in the scent bag to make it stand out, led them to the drop-off point.

Rafe jumped off Jeremy, happy to be back on the ground. He watched Jeremy shift to human, then report back that they were in position. He quickly shifted back to his wolf form. Rafe knew Jeremy was going to be pretty hungry when he got back after the numerous shifts.

They both settled in for the wait, all senses on the alert for anything which might be out there.

Chapter 37
1:00 AM

"Josh here. Rafe, time to start moving. Key your handset if you are on your way," the colonel's voice came over the earpiece.

Rafe reached back to press the tiny send button. It was awkward, but he depressed it, sending a clicking sound back to the others.

"OK. God's Speed. Call back once you're inside and in control of the control room. Josh, out."

Jeremy got to his feet. His taxi service and guard duty were at an end. Now he was to try and get back in time to join the others. He nuzzled Rafe in the direction of the compound.

Yeah, I know, I know. You don't have to push, Rafe thought.

He took a couple of steps forward. Sure that he was on his way, Jeremy slinked off. Rafe could hear his soft footfalls as he moved back and away.

I guess this is it!

Rafe started moving forward. There wasn't much cover the closer he got, and his rat instincts made him feel uncomfortable out in the open. And if someone was looking out for some reason, he didn't want to look like a rat with a purpose but rather a wandering rat looking for his next meal. So he moved forward in starts and stops, scurrying side to side as much as forward.

As he approached where he figured the sensors would be, his anxiety began to increase. Intellectually, he knew that he should be safe. These sensors picked up the vibrations of anything over 10 pounds moving by as well as anyone actually touching them. He was well below that weight threshold.

Finally, he could smell something which was out-of-place, man-made. Its scent was muted, as if it had been out in the elements for a long time. It had to be a sensor. Carefully approaching, he pinpointed its location, then moved to the side, and on rat tiptoes, he passed it. No alarms seemed to be raised. With a sigh of relief, he moved forward, locating the next one. They were actually a fair bit apart, further apart than he had expected. He wondered if Njaka could have made the passage, keeping exactly in the middle between each one. Surely the sensor field diminished a bit the further you got from the sensor itself?

He started his odd little tiptoe around another sensor, looking ahead and trying to make out the compound building ahead of him when he was suddenly jerked up, a piercing pain wracking his body. His mind was in total confusion as he twisted and gripped at the source of the pain. He could feel the wind rush by him as he suddenly realized that he was in the grasp of an owl. He didn't know how he could have let that happen. He tried to bite at the taloned foot which held him, but the owl was not letting go, and it was rapidly going to carry him off.

Idiot! he yelled at himself.

It only took a second to shift, and the owl suddenly had a full-grown human in its grasp. Or not. As soon as he shifted, Rafe tore free from the talons and fell to the ground. He landed with a thump, his breath knocked out of him.

Relief surged through him as he took inventory. He seemed to be in one piece. He looked up, but the owl had already vanished. Looking back, he could see the compound just 10 or 15 yards away. That meant he was still in the sensor field!

He heard a door slam above him. His body falling how many feet must have set off all the nearby sensors, and that door opening had to be people rushing to investigate. Almost without thinking, he shifted back to rat form and rushed forward to the edge of the compound wall. He could hear feet pound on the roof above him, and he tried to make himself mouse-small as a beam of light reached out into the night.

"You see anything?" boomed a voice directly above him.

"Nah, but let me look," came a higher pitched voice in reply.

The beam was bright enough for even Rafe's weak rat eyes to follow it as it searched and traversed the area.

"Doesn't look like anything. Probably another deer."

"All the way to the third band? Why didn't the outer two bands alert?" asked the second voice.

A dog's loud barks sounded right above him. Rafe should have sensed the dog with the two people, but he hadn't.

"What do you got there, Stag? Huh, boy?" the voice asked, the excitement in it raised a few notches.

Rafe could hear claws scramble for purchase on stucco, and some dog saliva fell just a few feet from him. The light was turned down and caught him dead to rights. He froze in place.

There was a laugh, followed by "You stupid dog! That ain't no werewolf. It's just a rat!"

The dog continued to bark and scrabble at the edge of the roof's retaining wall.

"Come on, boy, get back down before you fall."

"Pull him back, Steph. And let's get back down. I'll tell George to reset the alarms."

Rafe hadn't moved through the entire incident. He could hear footsteps retreating and the sound of claws on the roof above, as if the unwilling dog was being dragged against his will off the roof and back into the building. He felt he could finally let out a breath.

He still had to scale the wall and continue, but now he had a problem. When he shifted, his tiny gloves had basically exploded into pieces, and his carrier had broken apart as well. Now he was a naked rat, with nothing more than his body as a tool. He tried to peer into the sensor field to see if he could see any of his tools, but his eyes were not good enough for that. He had to have those things, though.

He ventured back out into the open, using his nose to see what he could find. It didn't take long before that led him to his carrier with the knife sheath, but the carrier was in pieces. There was no way it was going to fit back on him. The small ceramic knife was still in one piece, but without a carrier, he couldn't climb and carry it. He left it where he found it and continued casting about.

He found one small bootie, but it was in shreds. It wasn't going to stay on his paw without lots of repair, something Rafe couldn't do then and there. He was running out of time, and he couldn't search much longer. He was just about to give up when he found the earpiece lying in the grass. Gratefully, he pounced on it. His front paws were pretty dexterous, so without too much problem, he had fixed it in place. At least he had comms.

He bounded back up to the building. He wasn't sure quite where he was on the wall. The owl had moved him off course, and he couldn't see well enough to get the entire scope of it. And now, he had no gloves to keep him from contacting the silver in the sides of the building. He reached out a tentative paw to touch the wall and immediately jerked back as he was burned. How was he going to manage this?

He scurried along the base of the wall, searching for a way to get up. It all seemed the same to him, just this huge, looming barrier. A bit of motion caught his eyes, and he jumped back in alarm before realizing that it was only a rope or cable moving slightly in the breeze. Could this be his way up?

He rose up on his hind legs and tried to decipher what exactly it was. It seemed to come from the roof, then go into a small window on the second floor. But that meant there was still a good 12 or 15 feet from the ground to the cable. That was a long, long way.

He decided to keep moving. It didn't take long, though, until he reached the end of the building, and nothing presented itself to him. Time was getting shorter. He had to scale the wall and get into the control room.

He went back under the descending cable. He doubted that he could make it, but he had to try.

Rafe knew by now that he could jump about 3 feet straight up. But that would leave another 10 or more feet to go, 10 or more feet on a silver-treated wall. But there was nothing that could be done about that. Deciding a running start would be best, he backed up away from the building. He could barely make out the cable above him. He had to reach, it, though. Failure just wasn't an option.

Gathering himself, and before he could re-think things over, he sprinted forward and launched himself up. As he collided with the wall, a shock of burning pain washed over him like an explosion. His entire body was an agony of flames. He knew it would blow him right back off the wall, but he refused to go down without a fight. By pure force of will, he moved up the wall, not in the halting steps as in his rehearsal, but in one rushing moment. He moved up quickly, his mind lost in agony. He only peripherally felt himself lose contact with the rough stucco, but as he started to fall, one flailing paw caught a hold of something solid, something that didn't burn. He clamped his other paw on that then wrapped his entire body around that blessed anchor.

His mind was a mess. He couldn't think straight, and the pain threatened to overwhelm him. After a few seconds, a few minutes, or a few hours—he wasn't sure how long—his mind finally began to make some sense out of the world. And he realized that somehow, he had made the cable. He was clinging to a tv cable, one going in and disappearing under the small, closed window. He could see faint flickering coming from inside the room. Someone was watching television, even at this late hour.

Rafe was dizzy and nauseous. He wanted to drop back down on the ground and curl up somewhere to sleep. But he had to move forward. Going up the cable should have been easy, but Rafe almost had to will each paw to open and close. Step by agonizing step, always only an inch or two from the deadly wall, he made it up and to the satellite dish on the roof. At least the dish was free of any silver treatment. Rafe sat on the dish, trying to figure out where he was.

The plan had been for Rafe to scale the wall at the designated point, then go down the ventilation shaft there and make his way into the control room. Given the style of the heating system used, it should have been easy for a rat to make this journey. But as Rafe didn't know exactly where he was in relation to the correct shaft, he didn't know how to proceed.

Peering both right and left, he could make out the blurry shapes of two shafts. These were basically two tubes with small rain guards on top, from which exhaust from the heating and ventilation system left the building.

He gave himself a mental shrug. It probably wouldn't matter anyway as he thought he remembered that they were all connected. He was still feeling weak and disoriented, but he knew he had to move. Choosing the left shaft for no particular reason, he gathered himself to make the dash.

As before, he tried to jump as far as he could, but in his state, he barely moved forward before hitting the flat rooftop. He almost stopped right there as the agony threatened to overwhelm him. Fire took over his nerve endings. More to escape the unendurable pain than for concern for his mission, he charged forward to the shaft, somehow making it without losing consciousness. He climbed up the short shaft and squeezed beneath the rain guard. That was all he could manage, though, as he passed out and fell down the shaft to thud at the bottom of the metal ducting.

Rafe came to in stages, still feeling horrible, but blessing the cool metal of the ducting, metal which did not burn like hellfire. He wanted to lie there, out of touch with the ravages of his tortured little body. But his sense of purpose kicked in. Tabitha and Katie needed him. With an enormous effort, he hauled himself to his feet. He knew he was in the ducting which ran between the floors and took warm and conditioned air to the various rooms in this wing of the compound. But where was the control room?

Without rhyme or reason, he started making his way down the ducting. The first room grate he came to was to a dark room. He listened and smelled, but it was probably unoccupied. Occupied or not, though, this wasn't the control room. Very wobbly on his feet, he continued to the second grate. Even before he reached it, he could see light filtering down into the ductwork. This had more promise.

"This is Josh. Are you in the control room?"

The voice in his earpiece sounded loud, too loud. Rafe jumped back afraid anyone in the room above would certainly have to hear it. He reached up and keyed his handset twice for no.

Cautiously, he moved back forward until he could peer up through the grate. While he couldn't see the screens, the lights being emitted certainly looked like they belonged in a control room. He could smell someone in the room, as well. When that someone shifted and broke open what sounded and smelled like a potato chip bag, Rafe knew that someone was awake as well. This was it, then.

The grate consisted of a grill-like lattice, each opening barely bigger than a quarter. This might seem too small to let a rat through, but Rafe knew it was no real barrier. Taking care not to let his earpiece get scraped off, he pushed his way through one opening, and within moments, was in the control room. A huge man sat in a chair only a few feet away, but he didn't take notice of the intruder.

Rafe was afraid he was going to pass out. He certainly wanted to. His feet and parts of his body were blistered, and each step was more agony. But he had to take action.

Without his knife, Rafe wasn't sure how he would take on the guy on duty. He seemed enormous, but that could be just from Rafe's rat perspective. The man shifted in his chair, and Rafe jumped back. He had to gather himself! This was when he had to do what needed to be done. Thinking of Tabitha, he reached down to call back his human form and . . .

. . . nothing happened. He was still a rat. He tried again, and while there was a small stirring, he stayed a rat. He started panting with the effort. Nothing was working, and trying only brought more nausea. He had to stop.

Then he realized it. He was poisoned by the silver. He wasn't going to be able to shift. None of those who had been shot by silver in the last fiasco had yet been able to shift, even though the silver bullets had been taken out, and that was how many days ago? Rafe was stuck a rat for the foreseeable future.

So how was he going to take out the man, then flip the huge (to him) switches to turn off the sensors and the main gate? There was no way he could do it.

"Rafe, we're about ready out here. I hope you are, too, because we're starting in just a few."

Rafe keyed the handset twice. The rescue was going to be cancelled, and Tabitha was never going to be freed.

"I got that as a no. I don't know what is going on there. But you needed to get going. Remember what I told you. You have got to use all your tools, human and animal. Take what you have and make it work. We're kicking off in two minutes. Forget the sensors, if you have to. But if that gate isn't open, and if we can't ram our way in, I'm calling it off. So get it done. Josh out."

Rafe sat down in a decidedly human posture. That was it, then. He had failed. Use what you have? He had nothing. He was a rat. He had four small legs, a naked tail, whiskers, protruding teeth, a nose . . . teeth? He sat back up.

His teeth were pretty strong, right? Maybe he could bite the wiring? It was worth a shot.

Two minutes with a bit gone already. Another two minutes to the gate. Did he have time? He rushed to the power outlet. A normal rat could gnaw through that plastic cover in minutes, but he didn't have minutes. Could a wererat do it faster? Only one way to find out. He attacked the edge of the plastic cover with his paws and teeth. With a loud crack, a piece fell off, big enough for him to squeeze through.

He ignored the shout behind him as the crack roused the guy on duty. Scrambling up in the dark, he moved to where he thought the wires controlling the switches were. But which ones were which? Rats had some color ability, but not great, and in the darkness, he could discern even less. He grabbed one, then another. Time was fleeing.

He realized he could just go for the main. That would shut down everything. Of course, 110 volts, or more likely 220 for the main, running through him wouldn't do him any good, but if that would free the girls, then maybe this was his purpose in life.

The main cable was easily identified even to Rafe. It was larger cable leading into a junction box. That box then powered the room.

"Fifteen seconds, Rafe. I hope to God you've got the power off, because we're coming."

It was now or never. Rafe grabbed the power cable with his two front paws, and then with a short prayer, bit down will all his might.

The resultant explosion threw Rafe to the ground and out cold.

Chapter 38

The smell of burning hair slowly permeated Rafe's senses. What was that? He tried to clean off his whiskers to help get rid of the stench, but it didn't seem like he had any whiskers left. Was he back in human form?

He opened his eyes. No, he was still a rat. A badly burned rat. A small fire kindled in the crawlspace, and a hole had actually burned through the plasterboard, opening up a way into the control room. He knew he should get out into the more open area. Fires would kill a were, after all. But he didn't seem to have the energy.

He was vaguely aware of sounds from far, far away. They sounded like gunshots and screams, but that could just be in his imagination.

He could see out into the control room, now with only the overhead light providing illumination. All the screens were off. The door opened and legs strode in.

"Thank God, Anton! What's going on?" a fearful voice called out. It had to be the guy on duty.

"The demons have attacked, that's what's going on."

"But, I never, I mean, the alarms never sounded."

"They sounded once, didn't they?"

Even befuddled as he was, that voice reeked of evil intentions to Rafe.

"But Chance and Steph, they said that was nothing," was the plaintive reply.

"Obviously, it was. So I see we have no cameras working? None of the controls for the mines, either?"

"Everything's off. There was an explosion in the wall, then I lost everything. "

"Then what are you doing here? Get out and help turn the demons back."

There was a scrambling and Rafe could disinterestedly watch a rather wide backside of a person hurrying out the door. The other man, a man who piqued Rafe's muddled memory, stood there for a moment. Then he came forward to the smoldering hole in the plasterboard. He bent over and peered inside. Despite Rafe's confusion, he recognized that face. This was the man who had killed Claire. Anger welled inside of him, helping clear his head a bit, but not much else.

Anton Borisov reached in and grabbed Rafe, pulling him through the wall and out into the control room. Once he saw what he was pulling, he threw Rafe down in disgust, them jumped back.

"What cursed timing!" he shouted in anger.

He wiped his hand on his pants, then started to wheel about before he stopped, then swung back to look at Rafe. His eyes widened.

"What the . . . ?" He reached down again and touched the earpiece, still stuck over Rafe's ear. It had survived the shock and short circuit, maybe not working, but in one piece.

He stood back up, comprehension dawning.

"A rat? A wererat? That's, that's a first. And that's how you got in," he said to himself. And then to Rafe, who lay on the floor panting, "I almost have to admire you, and maybe I do. But that's not going to save you now. I'm going to send you to hell, now, before I go out and finish with your friends outside."

He pulled out a large silver knife, almost like a shortsword. With a gleeful look in his eyes, he moved forward to the wererat.

Rafe knew he was finished. But he also knew that his tribe was inside the compound. And he trusted that strange man, the colonel, to get things done. He wanted to let go, to just go to sleep, but this man in front of him ignited a deep-seated and long-held anger. This was the man who killed his sister. Rafe had watched him impotently from the tree as he had hacked with his silver-tipped pike at his sister, beheading her. Rafe watched this horror before running away naked back to the tribe, back to his self-imposed exile.

Something suddenly clicked in his mind. Naked? He had shifted back to his human form then. But how had he done that right after being silver-burned? Weres couldn't do that. But then again, weres usually couldn't second-shift on their own, either, not so soon after First Shift. Rafe had managed, that.

In another few seconds, Borisov was going to cut his body in half maybe, behead him maybe. Either way, his time on this earth would be over, and Anton would live to kill more of his people. And they were his people, despite the fact that he no longer lived with the tribe.

All of this flashed by in an instant, and in that instant, Rafe vowed it would not end like this. If he had shifted before while silver-burned, he could do it again. He reached deep down inside himself, deeper than he ever had before. He felt his human form, almost like an unresisting and unmoving lump of clay. He grabbed at it, pulling it. But it was stuck in a quagmire of some sort. It would not budge. He reached further within himself as Anton started to bring back his shortsword, calling forth resources he never thought he possessed. And finally, somehow, his body came. His eyes came to focus on an open-mouthed Anton, silver sword clattering to the floor. Anton took a step back as Rafe reached out and grabbed him by the neck.

Rafe was a somewhat of a UFC fan. He had sometimes imagined what it would be like to get into a fight, to finish it with a superman punch or naked guillotine. This was nothing like that. He put his big hands around the man's throat and started to squeeze. Anton reached up to grab his arms, but he couldn't budge them. His face became red and his eyes huge as he flailed.

A sudden excruciating pain blossomed in Rafe's side, and he could see the triumph spark in Anton's eyes, despite his deathhold on the man's neck. That triumph sputtered as Rafe merely tightened his hold to be replaced with fear. Even Rafe's human nose recognized the smell of urine as Anton let loose, moments before the life fled from his eyes and body.

Rafe kept squeezing. There would be no miraculous return to life for this vermin. His arms began to tremble, but still he held on, long after Anton was merely a slab of dead meat. Even as his dead body slumped to the ground, Rafe held on.

Finally, the pain in his side overwhelmed him. He looked down to see a small silver handle still in Anton's unfeeling hands. From his side, blood was pouring freely. He could just see a glint of the broken end of what had to be a silver blade which was stuck deep inside of him.

He let go of Anton, then slumped back. There were fewer sounds of gunfire now, but still some screaming and roars. His back began to burn, and it took him a moment to realize that that was not from silver, but from the fire. The flames inside the crawlspace had caught and turned into a blaze.

If it wasn't for the fire, Rafe might have just gone to sleep and passed on right there. But while fading away in his sleep had an allure, burning to death did not. He thought he had no more resources, but he surprised himself by finding a small reservoir of strength, and he managed to get to his feet. He stopped at Anton's dead body and removed his shoes. They were way too small for him, but he managed to slide his feet in as if they were slippers. The smoke was thick as he stumbled out of the room, never giving the dead Anton even one last glance.

He lurched down the hallway. He managed a smile as he realized that these people thought they were fighting werewolves, but he looked more like a zombie as he made his way to where the access stairwell to the roof was.

If it had been locked, that would have been too much for him. But the door was open. That made the stairwell pull like chimney, and the fire would soon engulf it, but for the moment, it was flame-free. Rafe pulled himself up the stairs, each step a laborious journey. When he stumbled, he was surprised to see that he had already made it outside. He was on the roof.

He moved to the inside wall. Looking out over the courtyard, he could see it was mostly over. There were a number of dead bodies lying on the ground, all clothed, so they were from God's Judgment. His eyes caught on a small body directly beneath him. It was a girl, maybe 10 or 11 years old. Her throat had been torn out, the blood soaking into the grass. He knew he should feel something, but he was just numb.

There was still fighting going on in the far wing. He couldn't see much, but he could hear. The flames started growing around him as a group of people and animals hurried to one of the rescue force's trucks. Rafe lunged forward despite the flames licking at him from below. There, in Mr. Peterson's arms, was the unmistakable shape of Tabitha. Despite the distance, the darkness, and the flames, Rafe was positive of that.

Tears coursed down his face. At least she was free. The heat finally drove him back. He looked down at the broken end of the silver blade in his side and idly picked at it. His fingers burned to match the burning in his side, but it didn't seem to hurt quite as much. Maybe his body was getting used to it. That or just shutting down.

He moved to the middle of the roof and stood there. The fire was surrounding him. He considered jumping off, and in his rat form, he would probably survive it. He wasn't sure if he could in his wounded human form. And he didn't have the energy, anyway.

A lash of fire suddenly struck him across the shoulder. Not the burn of silver, not the burning heat of the flames, but that of a clean slice. He looked up to see the shape of a golden eagle swooping by. It wheeled up, then came pelting down again. Rafe managed to get up his arm as the eagle slashed at him again. It was Alysha, he knew. And it looked like she wanted to finish him, to get her revenge for her dead husband. He managed a chuckle. She didn't have to do anything. He would be dead soon enough.

Alysha came down into a dive again, then swooped up right before she reached him. At the apex of her upwards swoop, she shifted in midair.

Her human body swung about as she shouted "Shift, you idiot!"

Immediately, she shifted back to her eagle form, great wings taking the strain of her previously increased falling mass. Rafe had never seen a raptor shift like that, although there were general rumors about that among the landbound weres.

Rafe's initial impression was that she wanted him as a rat in order to kill him. She should have no problem with that. But what if that wasn't her goal? Should he trust her? He looked around at the rapidly growing flames. Well, to stay here left a more certain ending to the world's only known wererat. And an eagle's clean talons sounded better than the flames' hungry bite.

Of course, shifting was more easily said than done. Before, when he shifted back to human form, he had only been burned. Now he had a silver blade stuck inside of him. Even if he could shift, what would happen to the blade in his suddenly tiny body? Would it cut him in two?

Alysha had gotten to the peak of one more climb and was beginning her dive back down towards him. Rafe tried to reach down and call forth his rat, but he didn't have the energy nor will. Tears began to flow as he felt the sorrow of really leaving this world, of not seeing his parents, Tabitha, MJ. It all seemed unfair. His whole life seemed unfair. He wanted a mulligan, a do over.

Alysha was coming down low over the building now, her flight interrupted by the flames' updrafts. This had to be her last chance at him.

As she swooped in, talons outstretched, Rafe gave in to himself, to his human, to his rat. This was who he was, no shame, but no pride either. This was how he was born, and this was how he would live. He embraced his rat.

And Alysha's talons closed about him, lifting him off the roof as part of it collapsed in the flames. Rafe felt the cool wind in his face as he faded in and out of consciousness, secure as the golden eagle carried him off.

Chapter 39
back in Rafe's bedroom, two days later

Rafe opened his eyes, wondering where he was. His mouth tasted like a sewer, and he ran his tongue over dry and cracked lips. He turned his head. Remy was standing there in the nightstand. It was his nightstand, so he must be back at home in his own bed. Remy looked the same as always, which seemed a bit surreal, given the last few days. He turned this head the other way, and there, curled up on his chair, was Tabitha. She was in a nightgown and a fluffy pink terrycloth robe, feet drawn under her butt, with her head back. Faint snores reached his ears.

He was back in his room, and Tabitha was sitting there, looking well. Relief washed over him. He wanted to jump up and hug her, but his body did not want to cooperate. He felt as weak as a kitten.

"Tabitha?" he managed to croak out.

She opened her eyes, then caught his. A huge smile blossomed as she jumped up and rushed to him, throwing herself on top and squeezing him for all she was worth. Rafe could feel hot tears falling onto his throat as she held him. He put his own arms around her, and while not as fiercely, hugged her back.

Finally, she backed off a bit, still holding him, but so she could look as his face.

"Hey, big brother," was all she said, tears streaking her cheeks.

"Hey, Tabby Cat."

Suddenly, she turned her head and shoulders around.

"Mom! Rafe's awake!" she shouted out the door. She turned back to him. "How're you feeling? You need anything?"

"A little water would be good."

His stomach took the opportunity to rumble.

"Maybe something to eat, too?" Tabitha asked with a laugh.

"Bring some food, too," she shouted out the door as she went back to the chair and got a half-empty can of Coke, bringing it to Rafe.

Rafe sucked it down. It was a little flat, but he didn't care.

"Are you OK? I mean, what did they do to you?" he asked, his voice a little stronger after the Coke.

She reached up to brush some hair on his forehead to the side. "I'm OK. Surprisingly, they didn't treat us too bad. Oh, we had a silver ankle band on the whole time, and that kept both of us pretty sick and in pain, but other than that, they didn't really abuse us. Physically, that is. Their constant preaching to us was pretty annoying." She brought up her leg to show Rafe the scarring just above her ankle. "Mr. Peterson thinks the scars might never heal, and I still feel kinda sick. I can't shift yet, and I think it's going to be awhile, but I'm OK."

His mother came in followed by Jaira. Rafe was happy to see his mother, but the sandwiches Jaira was carrying took his attention. He grabbed them and stuffed the first one, not even knowing what kind of sandwich it was, into his mouth before his mother could smother him with a hug.

"Rafe, I'm so glad you're awake. I've been worried about you."

He grabbed another sandwich as his mother released him from her grasp.

"How long have I been asleep?" he asked, between bites.

"Two days now."

Rafe stopped chewing. "Two days?"

"Yeah, two days. We got you home yesterday evening, and you've been asleep since then."

"What happened? I mean, I didn't see everything."

"Alysha flew back to the staging area with you, but you were pretty much out of it. We put you in with Tabitha in the van to come back. A couple of hours later, you just shifted back, but you were still out. When we got you back home, we just put you to bed and waited," his mother told him.

He remembered being lifted off the burning roof, but not much else. But he wanted to know more, not what happened to him.

"I mean, what happened to the assault? Is everyone OK?"

"It was a complete surprise. We think most of them were asleep when we hit them. When the colonel gave the order, we knew the gate and the sensors had not been neutralized, but we went anyway. Nothing was going to stop us, I think. But the gate was still open when we barreled through."

"Thanks to you," Jaira interjected.

"Yes, thanks to you," his mother agreed. "Well the sensors might have still gone off as we drove up, but they really didn't have much time to get prepared. We hit them hard. As soon as we piled out of the trucks, the entry teams shifted, took the battering rams off the bears, then took out the doors. It probably took, what, less than a minute to get in?" she looked around, continuing after Jaira nodded her agreement. "Then it was just going berserk in the halls and rooms. If anyone came out, well, we killed them."

There was a short pause at this. People had died. But looking at both his mother and Jaira, he didn't see any regret, but rather a look of retained excitement. Rafe wondered how many people his mother had killed, how many throats she had torn out. Someone had killed a young girl. Could his mother have done that?

"Anyway, it took our rescue team longer to find the girls. They weren't where we figured them to be. They were being held in their chapel, in the sacristy. So it took some time to find them."

"And there were no problems there?"

"Well, we had an ally, sort of," Tabitha said. "Our guard was this guy who took care of us a lot. And he talked to us. I don't think he really wanted to hurt us, and even though the ghoul gave the order to kill us if it looked like we could be rescued, well, Scott couldn't do it. When the others came in, he just unlocked us and let us go."

"Trying to save his own hide, I'm sure," his mother added sourly.

"I don't think so, Mom. I think he was just raised in this group and knew nothing else. But he couldn't really accept everything told to him."

"Well, it worked for him. Katie kept Shelly from killing him, and he's still alive now."

Rafe could tell from her tone that she wasn't happy about that.

"'The ghoul?'" asked Rafe.

"Yeah, that's what Katie and me called their boss, Mr. Anton. He took over when the old guy, the deacon, died last year. We don't know what happened to him, though." She shuddered as she said that last.

"He's dead," Rafe told them.

"You saw him? You saw him actually dead?" asked Tabitha in an excited and hopeful voice.

"I killed him."

He grabbed another sandwich and started eating it. Tuna, he realized. Jaira had put in the sweet pickles he really liked, and used Miracle Whip instead of mayonnaise. Instead of talking about killing a man, he might as well as been talking about going to a movie or taking a walk, for all the emotion it brought up.

The other three just stared at him while he ate, mouths open in surprise. He peeled open one edge of the sandwich and peered inside, then smiled with pleasure before closing it and taking another bite.

"Anybody there?" a voiced called from downstairs.

"Jaira, that's Colonel Hartigan. Can you go bring him up?" his mother broke the silence.

As Jaira left to get him, Tabitha took his hand, stopping him from bringing the sandwich back up to his mouth.

"You sure, Rafe? You really killed him?"

"Yep."

"Damn, that's great!"

She sat on the edge side of the bed, maybe unconsciously presenting a united front with Rafe as the colonel came in the room.

"You OK, son?" he asked, without preamble.

"Yes, sir, colonel. I'm fine."

The man rolled his eyes. "Why do you all insist on calling me 'colonel?'"

"Well, because you are a colonel," Rafe told him.

"I was a colonel. I'm retired from that now. And I keep telling you my name is Josh." He looked at their blank faces. "Look, does everyone call your mom 'Dr. Turner?'" He nodded towards her, but kept his attention on Rafe.

"No, of course not."

"But she has a Ph.D., right?"

"Well, yeah, I guess so."

"So why don't you call people how they want you to call them. And for me, that's Josh." He paused. "But what am I doing prattling on about names? Now that you're awake, I need you to fill in some holes for me so I can make my report. I need to know what happened. Tank did a recon the morning after, and he found your carrier, your knife, your shirt, and three of your booties out in the grass behind the compound. So you didn't have them when you infiltrated?"

"No, sir." He went on to explain how the owl had caught him, causing him to have to shift. They stood in silence as he went on to describe his scaling the wall and what that did to him.

The colonel looked at him in awe. "You mean, you climbed the wall without protection? In contact with the silver in it?"

"Yes, sir."

"Amazing! Then what happened?"

Rafe went on with his narrative. As he described biting through the power cable, both his mother and the colonel sat down at the foot of the bed.

"You could've been killed," she exclaimed weakly.

When he got to the point where he was on the floor, Borisov getting ready to kill him, Tabitha burst out, "And that's when you killed him?"

"But Rafe, how could you? I mean, we needed you to get in the building, so your animal form was useful, but against an armed man? I mean, no disrespect, but . . ?" his mother asked.

Rafe looked at the colonel. "You told me how, sir."

"I did?"

"Yes, sir. You told me to use all my resources, to use what I had. So I shifted back and strangled him with my bare hands. He stabbed me with a knife . . ." he reached down to rub the scar tissue where the knife had entered him, ". . . but I just kept squeezing until he was dead."

"You shifted after being silver-burned, after almost blowing your head off? And you kept throttling him even with a silver knife in your side? How could you do it?"

"I had to."

"And that explains why Alysha said you wouldn't shift back to your rat form at first when she tried to pull you off the roof. You had a silver blade in you. But you did manage to shift in the end."

"Well, like I said, I had to."

"I think, son, that some people, including me, I'm ashamed to admit, have been underestimating you. We're going to have to talk more on this later."

Rafe was feeling rather uncomfortable with all the attention. They spoke some more, but he was grateful when the colonel had to leave. He told his mother that he was getting a bit tired, so she and Jaira reluctantly left.

"Where's Dad?" he asked Tabitha when it was only the two of them.

Her eyes clouded over. "He's not doing so well. He's in bed now, but I'm sure he'll be in to see you soon."

That saddened him. He had an image of his father, the strong, laughing man. He hoped that man could make it back.

He and Tabitha chatted for awhile, but then he really was tired. Finally, Tabitha left him, but not before taking Remy off the nightstand and placing him beside Rafe. He thought that was a little childish, but it still felt comforting as he drifted off to sleep.

Chapter 40
a week later

Rafe came back into the house from his walk. He had recovered much faster than he had been told to expect. He had also managed to shift several times, again much sooner than he had told he would be able to do that. He hadn't stayed in form and spent any time as a rat; he just wanted to see if he could shift.

He had called MJ to tell her he was sick and would be a little longer. MJ had taken it well, as he expected, but his academic advisor had gotten somewhat on his case, telling him he was endangering his enrollment.

Today, he had left the house for the first time since the rescue. It had been good to get out in the sun, to get some fresh air. Tabitha had tried to insist on going with him, but he needed the time alone.

Not that he had too much time alone. As he walked, a number of people either came up to shake his hand or merely wave hello. That was more attention than he had had from the tribe in years. He had avoided the community center, but even on the side streets, he was far from alone.

Turning one corner, he was surprised to see Trevor hurrying up to him. He braced himself.

"Turner! I need to talk to you."

Rafe sighed and stopped. He thought it was better to get this over with sooner rather than later. He knew Trevor wanted him gone, but didn't his actions in the rescue earn him a breather?

Trevor reached him and stopped.

"Look, Turner. I mean look, Rafe. We all know what you did. Josh told us. And, well, we think you did great. And, well . . ." He stopped and looked at the sky with an expression of exasperation on his face.

"Look, I'm shitty at this kind of thing. I've been an ass to you. And those things I said to you before, well, forget them. You're welcome to stay here as long as you want. And I would be honored to shake your hand."

Rafe took the proffered hand out of instinct, but then shook it with purpose.

"We cool?" Trevor asked.

"Well, you've been an ass, true. But yeah, 'we cool.'"

A smile broke over Trevor's face as he let go of Rafe's hand to pound him on the shoulder.

"Great. I mean it. We want you to stay. If you need anything, give me a shout. And oh, yeah, we're going out to get a beer later on. Why don't you come along?"

"OK, maybe I will."

Rafe had watched Trevor stride off. He didn't know how he felt about this sea change, but it had to be better than what he had before.

He was still contemplating this when he walked back into the house. He didn't want to go back up to his room yet, so he went straight into the kitchen to see if there was something he could steal before dinner.

"Rafe, is that you?" his mother called out from the family room. "Can you come here?"

"Yeah, mom, just a sec."

He grabbed a chocolate chip cookie and went to see his mom. He was surprised to see another man there. His long black hair, eagle nose, and Native American-patterned shirt indicated that he probably was a Native American.

"Rafe, I want you to meet David Marten."

David Marten? Rafe hurried over to shake the man's hand.

"So this is the famous wererat," he said with a smile cracking his weathered face.

"Uh, yeah." Rafe might have bristled a bit at that, but David Marten was the world's only werebeaver, so that made things different.

"So, we're brother rodents, huh? Good to meet you, and great to see that not all of our people are stuck with muscle-bound bodies."

Rafe had read about people with a "twinkle in their eyes," but this was the first time he had actually seen it. He took an immediate liking to the man. Rafe felt that liking went above and beyond the fact that of anyone, this man would know what it was like to be like him. And this man was pretty well-respected.

"What are you doing here?" Rafe asked.

"I'm here for a couple of reasons. Maybe to meet you? A fellow wererodent?"

"No, I mean really?"

"Well, you're part of the reason. Not the only reason, but still, part. Let me ask you, what do you think of Josh Hartigan?"

"The colonel?" Rafe thought for a bit. "Well, I admire him, I guess. I don't think we could've rescued my sister and Katie without him."

"Well, he was rather impressed with you, I have to say. And he's asked if he can take you under his wing. He wants you to be his apprentice, so-to-speak. What do you think about that?"

"Wow! Me?"

The idea threw him for a loop. Someone wanted him? That was a unique feeling. But did he want that? Could he run around for the United Tribes, putting out fires? He wasn't sure. He looked to his mother, then to Mr. Marten.

"I am really flattered, but I'm not sure. I killed a man with my hands, and while I have no regrets, I'm not sure I want to do that again."

Mr. Marten nodded. "Fair enough. Think about it, though, because the offer will be open for awhile."

"How do you know, this, though? Why are you asking me this?" Rafe asked, curiosity raising its head.

"Well, that's another thing. Your mother here. . ." he stopped to look at her. "You sure about this, Ann?"

"I think it's time, David. And Hank's going to need me. So yes, I'm sure." She didn't sound so sure, though.

Mr. Marten turned back towards Rafe. "You're not supposed to know this, but your mother is a member of the United Tribes Council. Well, has been a member. She just resigned."

Rafe took a step back in shock and surprise? His mother? Then, as he started to think about it, it sort of made sense. She was always in the family-room-cum-office, doing far more work than her part in running the tribe should have taken. But it was still a shock. Then he looked up at Mr. Marten.

"Then that means, you. . . "

"Yes, I'm on the Council, too," he said with a laugh. "Now, who is on the Council is not really Top Secret, but almost so. So we are trusting you to keep this to yourself. People like Josh work directly for us, but even he doesn't know who we are. He didn't know your mom was a member, for example."

"So what's all this got to do with me?"

"Right to the point. Well, OK. There isn't a quota, per se, of from which tribes each Council member comes from. But there is a bit of politics involved, and with your mother resigning, well, I'm willing to put your name forward."

"But I'm not a leader. I don't even live here anymore."

"True enough. But you're a bit of a hero now, and you've evidently got some skills which are impressing other members. But even if they are amazed by the reports on your abilities to shift, the bottom line is that except for me, almost all of the other Council members were nominated based on their strength as a were, on how big and ferocious they were. And with that, no matter what, they aren't going to be concerned with a mere rat. You won't be a threat. And with time to season, you, and me, of course, as your equally unassuming mentor, can use that to our advantage."

He looked impressed with his own logic. It made sense to Rafe, too, in a way. But a member of the Council? Would he ever really be free to be himself again? On the other hand, the honor was huge, and rat or not, he could have an impact upon his people.

"I don't know what to say, sir. This is pretty sudden. Can I think about it for a bit?"

"Sure, Rafe. You need to do this because you think you can do some good in the position, not for the glory, of which there isn't much, to be sure. But don't wait too long. We need to nominate someone within the next couple of weeks."

"And with that, Ann, I really need to get going. I've got a plane to catch."

They both hugged each other and kissed cheeks. After they broke apart, Mr. Marten held out a hand to Rafe.

"I hope to hear back from you soon."

Rafe and his mother walked him out, then waved as he drove off in his rental car. His mother kept a hand on his shoulder as they watched him leave. She turned to give him a hug.

"You know, Rafe, I'm so proud of you. It's going to be great to have you back here at home, where you belong."

Rafe pondered that as he walked up the stairs a few minutes later. Was this his home? It had been his home, true. But so had the road, the Portland streets, the Porch Light Youth Shelter, Oregon State, and now UC San Diego. These were his people, though, and blood was both a duty and a calling. He seemed to be accepted now, and that was what he wanted, right?

He walked into his room. His folks had left it pretty much the way it had been when he had left. If he could go back in time to the day he left, or rather, just before he left, he would. Claire would still be alive and his world would be different. But Claire was still dead, murdered. Rafe had gotten his revenge and helped save his little sister, but that did not bring back his big sister.

Remy stood staring at him, back up on his stand on the nightstand. The blue rat seemed to look into his soul. "Anyone can cook," Chef Gusteau had told him, and then Remy had done just that. He hadn't let being a rat keep him from who he was.

And all this time, Remy had been telling him the same thing. Not about cooking, but about accepting and being yourself. The colonel had basically said the same thing as well and had used him as a weapon. But Remy's message seemed more real, more poignant.

Rafe was Rafe. He wasn't a rat, although a rat was him. He wasn't the son of a Council member, although that was him, too. He wasn't a masters student, nor a street kid, but they were him as well. He couldn't let others' expectations of him rule his world.

He walked over and picked up the stuffed blue toy. He stared into the plastic eyes.

"I get it, little chef. I get it."

He walked out the door and down to Tabitha's room. She was out, but he didn't need her there. He placed Remy in the middle of her bed. Remy had helped him come to grips with himself, and Rafe didn't need him anymore. He knew who he was.

Epilogue

Rafe pulled into the parking lot. He sat in the car for a moment, gathering his thoughts. It had been a long few weeks. Physically, he had pretty much healed. But mentally, he felt he had gone beyond and transcended where he had been before he left for his Gammy's funeral. Before he had left the tribe, in fact. He felt at ease with himself and his future, of what he was going to do with his life. Finally, he was happy with whom he was.

He got out of the car, reached back for his backpack, and locked the doors. Slinging one strap over one arm, he let the pack dangle as he approached the building. His pulse picked up as he walked up the steps. He had made his choice, and he was about to embrace his future. This is what he was meant to do.

He walked down the hallway until he stood in front of the door. Once he opened it, his path was set. He still had other options, but in his heart, he knew this was the right choice.

Fumbling in his pocket, he took out the keys and opened the door.

"MJ, I'm home!"

Jonathan P. Brazee

If you would like updates on new books releases, news, or special offers, please consider signing up for my mailing list. Your email will not be sold, rented, or in any other way disseminated. If you are interested, please sign up at the link below:

http://eepurl.com/bnFSHH

Other Books by Jonathan Brazee

The Return of the Marines Trilogy
The Few
The Proud
The Marines

The Al Anbar Chronicles: First Marine Expeditionary Force--Iraq
Prisoner of Fallujah
Combat Corpsman
Sniper

The United Federation Marine Corps
Recruit
Sergeant
Lieutenant
Captain
Major
Lieutenant Colonel
Colonel
Commandant

Rebel
(Set in the UFMC universe.)

Women of the United Federation Marines
Gladiator
Sniper
Corpsman (working title)

Werewolf of Marines
Werewolf of Marines: Semper Lycanus
Werewolf of Marines: Patria Lycanus
Coming: Book Three

To The Shores of Tripoli

Wererat

Darwin's Quest: The Search for the Ultimate Survivor

Venus: A Paleolithic Short Story

Non-Fiction

Exercise for a Longer Life

Author Website
http://www.jonathanbrazee.com

www.ingramcontent.com/pod-product-compliance
Lightning Source LLC
Chambersburg PA
CBHW070853120626
46556CB00002B/976